SHAPE THE BLACK SKY

Christopher Dwyer

iUniverse, Inc.
New York Lincoln Shanghai

Shape The Black Sky

iUniverse books may be ordered through booksellers or by contacting:

iUniverse
2021 Pine Lake Road, Suite 100
Lincoln, NE 68512
www.iuniverse.com
1-800-Authors (1-800-288-4677)

ISBN: 0-595-34439-9

Printed in the United States of America

SHAPE THE BLACK SKY

Acknowledgements

For Kat, Nunnie, Aunt Lucy, Baby Nicky, Baby Marco, Il Babbo, Mother Angela, Lisa, Uncle Marc, Danny, Charity, Adam and Mirza. Special thanks to Ryan Fielding for being the best friend a guy could have, as well as the most gifted literary consultant a writer could ever need.

PROLOGUE

▼

The ravenous moans of the undead continued outside. They continued to bang on the wooden door of the shop, each strike a twinge in Hilda Bentlon's heart.

She peered over at the body of her father, who was standing a few feet from the window, glancing outside. His eyes were fixated on their arms, gaping forward towards their prey. He put his head down and whispered something to himself.

Hilda gripped the pen near the shopkeeper's desk and searched for a paper. She found a stack of parchment on the nearby desk. Her father told her to keep the bulky piece of wood in her hand for protection, however, she traded the object for a pen.

As Hilda's father began to panic, she scrawled words on the paper, each one a frosty extension of the terror at hand.

As the shop door broke in pieces, Hilda continued to write. Her father screamed a few feet away before they attacked him.

CHAPTER 1

─────────────▼─────────────

It was raining again. Big, bombastic drops of water were hitting the window right above his bed. Tossing and turning, he was caught in yet another of those dreams.

In that netherworld, all that he ever wanted was at his fingertips, however, there was only one thing he truly yearned for: her touch. Whatever the dream encompassed, the end result was always the same. Reality was nowhere to be seen.

This was a typical scenario for Dez Cylan. It had been nearly two months since Koral had broken up with him, but the dithering feeling of loss and pain was as fresh as it could possibly be.

"I'm not in love with you," she had said on that sunny spring day. The words now echoed through Dez's skull like an oath of anguish and torture.

His life did not necessarily revolve around her, but at times it felt as if she was the only thing that mattered to him in this existence. And now, while his heart was attempting to slowly slither back to a realm of normalcy, nightly dreams of Koral had found a permanent place in his head, haunting his one true escape from the real world.

Dez lived in Revmont, a small suburb outside of Boston, while Koral was located in the Midwest. Long-distance relationships are usually destined for failure, many would say, but he didn't care. Koral had made an impermeable impact on the young Bostonian; the word "soulmate" was thrown around so much he honestly believed their relationship was something straight out of a campy romance novel.

Dez had spent the past two months wallowing in his misery. To him, hope of moving on was a trail lined with endless drinking. Partying wasn't going to help; his heart was broken, and there was nothing that could possibly fix that.

The rain hit the window pane harder as Dez attempted to slide back into slumber. Although he had nowhere in particular to go in the morning, lying in bed protruded the grief deeper into his mind, convalescing an aura of despair in which he had experienced so much in his short life.

*   *   *   *

It was sometime around 10 a.m. when Nathan turned on the shower. He thought of waking up his older brother up, but that would usually result in one of two different scenarios. Dez would either welcome the invitation, or throw an empty bottle of Bud Light at the door.

Nathan was worried about his brother. Ever since Koral and Dez split in late April, he felt that the brotherly bond they had once consistently experienced was drowning in a sea of conflicted confusion.

As Nathan began to lather his hair, he silently wished for an end to Dez's depression. He thought of the good times the two had over the past year. No matter how close to their respective friends and significant others, the value of brotherhood was one of a deep notion.

Nathan was only 19, but still felt important in his brother's life. Ever since the two had moved out of their parents' house, he honestly believed that there was nothing that was going to get in the way of having a best friend in his sibling.

At Christmas, Dez had bought him a brand new bass drum for his kit. The two would spend hours at each end of the spare room in the apartment, with Dez churning out blazing metal riffs while Nathan seared through double-timed drumming and frequent crashes of the cymbals.

As Nathan stepped out of the shower, he caught a glimpse of a guitar pick that his brother must have dropped on the bathroom floor. He realized that the two had not jammed in almost three months.

Nathan heard the refrigerator door slam, and figured that Dez had probably woken up after fighting the distraction of consistent shower noise.

"Dude, next time you wake up at the ass crack of dawn, do me a favor and take a *bath*," said Dez, wiping orange juice from his face and brushing his black bangs out of his face. His hair had gotten a tad bit longer in the past two months, Nathan had noticed.

"Listen, while you're in there acting like a depressed little boy, the world *does* continue to move on, you know," said Nathan, as he reached for one of his green work shirts.

"Whatever, bro. Are you going to work soon?" asked Dez.

"Yeah, I'm working an 11 to 6 today in grocery." Nathan had kept his high school job at Revmont's biggest supermarket, and made the decision to avoid college at all costs. He saw how hard his brother worked to get a Bachelor's degree, and how he went from being a "somebody" at college, and now resides as a "nobody" who spends hours a day playing the same four chords on an electric guitar while pining over the loss of love in the corner of his room.

Nathan headed out the door, and Dez headed back to his room. It was nearly 11 a.m., and the older of the two decided it was time try something new: face the outside world.

*   *   *   *

Dez thought he had gotten rid of all traces of Koral. The day she ended the relationship, he had packed everything that reminded him of her into two huge plastic bags and tossed them into storage.

He remembered the pain that encompassed his chest as he threw her 20-year-old teddy bear into the bottom of the dirty bag, along with framed pictures, CDs, sweaters and t-shirts, and a scrapbook that she had made him for his birthday last year.

Dez never thought that the torn blue fur of that teddy bear would ever see another home besides the foot of his bed. Now, it was somewhere near a leaky pipe in the apartment complex's basement.

It wasn't odd that he'd find minute items that were strewn amongst hidden corners in his room over the past couple months. Last week he had found a Radiohead album that she had given him a week after they had started dating. Into the barrel went the eclectic five-piece's CD without processed thought.

Dez leaned over the side of his bed to grab his cell phone. He had two new voicemails. One was from Johnny, no doubt.

Johnny and Dez met each other in elementary school. Although the two were speckled amongst opposite sides of the social spectrum, in their case, popularity did not reign supreme.

In high school, Johnny discovered punk rock, while Dez started toying with the idea of starting a metal band in his father's garage. Music was something the two had shared for what seemed like forever nowadays. Dez could vividly remember sitting in Johnny's 1987 black Monte Carlo in high school, blaring Mötley Crüe's *Shout At The Devil* album while cruising up and down Revmont Beach.

Dez and Johnny had gone through their share of problems over the past few months. While Koral encouraged nothing but the wealth of close friendships, especially in the wake of dealing with a constant "missing" feeling for her boyfriend, Dez inadvertently pushed his focus on his relationship with her rather than paying attention to his best friends.

Luckily for the sake of a childhood friendship, those problems withered away when the two shared a bottle of Jagermeister right after Dez's split with Koral.

The other voicemail was from a newspaper in Western Massachusetts. Dez had heard the story before. The phrase "we have no open staff positions" was something that he had known all too well. Post-collegiate life seemed promising before Dez had graduated. In the months that followed commencement, he had gotten caught up in what seemed like an easy life.

"Hey dude, wanted to see if you were up for some drinking tonight, give me a call back," said Johnny in his voicemail.

There'd be no drinking tonight, thought Dez. Whether he was at a bar or pounding beers in the apartment, the end result was always the same: waking up with loneliness and the severity of being without Koral.

Dez put on his jogging pants and a faded, old U2 shirt. Jogging was sometimes a trivial way to make himself feel better. It wasn't that he didn't feel attractive, it was just that his self-esteem was shattered into a million pieces. What female in her right mind would want a self-loathing, pathetic, unemployed guy like him? If there was one thing he missed, it was hearing that Koral loved his body.

He started to reminisce. Random thoughts came and went within his mind. Thoughts of her dark red hair, her smile, walking along Navy Pier in Chicago, hearing her say "Hi, my love." He had to stop doing this to himself. Let's just go for a jog, he thought.

Dez grabbed his keys and CD player and headed downstairs. *The Boston Herald* lied in front of his mailbox. He scanned the front page quickly. Something about church closings, something going on with Venus, and a big picture of Pedro Martinez from the Red Sox loss last night. Fucking Red Sox, he thought, as he began his jog along the busy street.

The cool June breeze whistled past his face as he turned the corner near City Hall. Dez realized that his pace had picked up significantly as the music pouring into his eardrums became more aggressive. Metallica was appropriate running music. "Fuck it all and no regrets" screamed James Hetfield as permeable pallets of sweat dripped into Dez's eyes.

He passed a group of elderly women waiting for the bus. As he rounded the corner after the benches near the bus stop, Dez paused to take a breath. As he huffed huge gasps of Revmont air, a large German Shepard walked past him. He patted the dog and started to jog again.

*　　　*　　　*　　　*

The Savionaire Rehabilition Center wasn't a pleasant place. It consisted of three floors, each filled with mentally handicapped patients. The SRC wasn't necessarily considered a hospital, however, at times it felt like one.

Chester looked at his watch. It was only 1:15. Lunch in 45 minutes, he thought.

"Huh-lo Ches-ter," said a big, hunchback-looking black man across the way from Chester.

"Hey buddy, how you doing today?" asked Chester as he fiddled with the change in his left front pocket.

"Um, I'm, um, fine," said the large character.

Chester felt bad for the poor guy. Taylor suffered from acute brain damage, and had spent the last 12 years at the SRC. His brain was damaged at birth, while the mother had passed on three hours later from loss of blood. Taylor was bounced around various group homes before he ended up at the SRC.

"Taylor buddy, you should get back to your room before someone sees you," said Chester."

"O-kay Ches-ter," said Taylor, bringing his attention to a Snickers bar left out on the counter. He grabbed the candy bar, and skipped back to the other side of the building. Chester smiled and looked at his watch again. It was only 1:21.

Chester Lavarsum, please report to Room 224. Chester Lavarsum, Room 224.

Fuck, thought Chester. It was probably another patient that snapped at a nurse and had to be tranquilized.

He ran up the stairs and onto the second floor. The second floor was known to the SRC's staff as the epicenter of violent patients. Almost every hour, Chester got a call to help sedate one of the SRC's 120 patients. He was never comfortable sticking a needle into the leg of a mentally handicapped individual; usually a fiery strike of guilt and shame encompassed him every time he had to sedate one of them.

Chester reached into his messenger bag for the small vial of tranquilizer and a syringe as he walked into Room 224. He looked around and saw Betty, the 55-year-old nurse who had perhaps the worst attitude of any woman on the planet, and Chuck, a 6 foot 6 bald man with so many disorders Chester couldn't count them all on both hands.

Betty was about 5 feet away from Chuck, who was swinging a metal cafeteria tray at the frightened nurse.

"Chuck, calm down. Give me back the tray," enticed Betty. "Chester, give me a hand here."

"Sure thing babe." Chester attempted to slowly move towards the patient. "Take it easy, fella, I'm not going to hurt you."

Chester leaped to the side of Chuck. The patient took a swing at him, but Chester ducked and edged the syringe into his side. Chuck let out a bellow and fell to the ground. Within minutes, the once violent giant was curled into a fetal position on the dirty tile floor.

Betty let out a sigh of relief. "Thanks for taking so long to get up here. That maniac could have bludgeoned me to death with that tray," she said.

"Oh, calm down honey, and make sure he doesn't end up spending the night on the floor," said Chester as he removed the needle from Chuck's side. "I'm going to grab some supplies from the back room. And so help me God, if I get any calls on my lunch break…"

"You're so pleasant, Chester."

Chester blew a kiss at the older nurse and headed to the third floor. She really needs to get laid, he thought, as he neared the staircase.

The medical supply room was almost always abandoned. There were supply closets on each floor, but what Chester *really* needed was kept in this room. Although he had been addicted to meth for almost six months now, he had assured himself that the habit was under his control.

Chester was not your typical meth addict. Which is why, of course, no one except his close friends knew he was addicted to the drug. Premature aging and rotting teeth were the signals of textbook cases, however, Chester exhibited none of these coarse qualities.

A medical supply room visit wasn't just for getting his fix, it was also a chance to soak up a variety of drugs into his bag for his own use, or for "trading" with local dealers. In one fell swoop, he stole a few bottles of vicodin. He never took more than a small amount, for fear of higher-ups or coworkers finding out.

He had to do this quickly. It had been almost four hours since he had last sniffed any, and he started itching for some right before the sedation call. He reached into his back pocket and pulled out a small, rolled up silver package. He peered out the window of the supply room. Like always, there was no one there. When Chester was at his apartment, he could light up a pipe and smoke what he needed. At work, however, he needed it to be a simple process. With one quick motion, Chester snorted the small line of meth off the five-shelf cabinet in front of him. His eyes rolled back into his head as a euphoric wave of pleasure gripped his body.

CHAPTER 2

▼

Dez fumbled for his keys in his pocket. He was tired, hot, and sweaty and was dying to take a shower. He opened the door to his apartment and threw down the CD player on the couch.

He walked into the bathroom and stared at himself in the mirror. He saw the distress in his own eyes. Dez wondered when the last time anyone had seen him smile. His face was getting scruffy, but he didn't care. He remembered back to when Koral used to jokingly complain about how she didn't like kissing him when his face was unkempt.

Dez looked down and tried to collect himself. He turned on the shower and undressed. It felt relieving to have the cool water placate his body. He let the steady stream of water relieve the tension in his face before he even started washing himself.

Stepping out of the tub, he grabbed for the blue towel on the rack. He had a vision of being in the shower with Koral. He missed sneaking up behind her while she was drying her hair to give her a hug and seeing a huge smile appear on her face.

Dez heard his cell phone ring. He ran into his bedroom and picked it up. It was Johnny.

"Dude, what's up?" asked Dez.

"Hey man, I left you a voicemail this morning. Where were you?"

"I went out for a jog. I just got back a little while ago."

"Cool, cool. I take it you're *not* up for some drinking later?"

"Honestly, no. But you and Chester are more than welcome to swing by here and hang out if you want. The Sox game is on, and I'm sure there's some beer in the fridge."

"Sounds good, man. I'll drop by around eight. I'll call Chester."

"Ok bro. Later."

A little company couldn't hurt, thought Dez. For the past two months, to the best of his ability, he tried to keep his head up and live life in the most normal methods. However, it was tough for him to be able to socialize with whoever he came across; Koral was the only thing on his mind.

He sat down to his desk in the living room and turned the computer on. Dez checked his email quickly, popped in some music album, and leaned back in his chair. What am I doing, he thought. Everyday was the same to Dez. He'd wake up every morning after having the same type of dream. He'd go for a jog, shower, and then check his email. Having the same routine wasn't helping him move on.

Dez got out of his chair and began to frantically pace around the living room. He began to inhale behemoth gasps of air and felt a slight twinge in his stomach. Another panic attack, he thought.

He sat back down in the plushy office chair next the computer. Dez started to dry-heave, and ran to the bathroom. He flipped up the toilet seat and ducked his head down as his throat jerked waves of vomit into the porcelain bowl. Hefty beads of sweat colluded on his forehead as the veins in his face constricted tighter and tighter.

In a sudden motion, Dez threw his head back and sat on the cold bathroom floor. In what seemed like forever, he slowly brought himself up to his feet. He looked in the mirror. Half of his jet black hair was soaked with toilet water, and the rest was tossed around in a messy fashion.

Dez looked closer at the gloomy figure in the mirror. His eyes were completely bloodshot. He turned on the cold water and filled his hands with water. Dez splashed his face and picked up a towel to dry his hair.

Panic attacks were not an everyday affair for Dez. Over the past two months, he had a wide array of emotions that either taunted him or drove him further into the unloving rut in which Koral had left him. These panic attacks came at awkward moments for Dez. The last one he had was the previous week at a bar in downtown Boston.

Dez remembered the incident clearly. He was standing next to a table in the corner of Big Jim's Bar and Grill. Chester and Johnny were arguing over which Guns 'N' Roses ballad had the best guitar solo. One of those trendy new garage bands was blaring from the jukebox. Dez was staring into nowhere with his dark brown eyes.

With an ice cold grip on his bottle of Bud Light, he had a vision of Koral looking up at him and smiling. She was almost six inches shorter than him. That made for the best hugs, she had always said. After taking a swig of beer, Dez started choking on the chilly liquid inside of his mouth and began to gasp for air. His eyes rolled back into his head and he blacked out.

The bar incident clamored feelings of frustration in Dez's head as he sat down on the worn out leather sofa in the living room. I can't believe that I'm letting that bitch get to me this much, he thought. "There must be a better life than this," he said aloud to the empty apartment.

He looked at the clock next to his "Dawn of the Dead" poster on the wall. It was almost three in the afternoon. The sun was shining brightly outside, but Dez didn't care. For a second, he reminisced to chatting with Koral on his cell phone outside of the apartment.

Last summer was incredible, he thought as he winced at the calendar in the kitchen. With a sharp and extended sigh, he realized that it was one year ago tomorrow that she had made her first official trip to Boston to visit him. Dez's mind vanished into a flood of memories. He thought of waiting at the baggage claim at Logan Airport for her. He remembered the brawny hug they shared when he greeted her. He remembered eating Chinese food that afternoon with Johnny and his girlfriend.

Dez thought back to the first time he had made love to Koral. Comedy Central was on the television. He missed her large, soft breasts as they bounced up and down. He remembered how she would lay face down after sex. Her face beat red, her body shaking, she would always say "I love you" before curling up with Dez.

Dez sighed again and ripped the calendar off the wall. He grabbed an empty beer bottle from the sink and heaved it at the wall. As the brown bottle smashed into many tiny pieces on the tiled kitchen floor, Dez sat down at the rectangular table and began to cry.

*   *   *   *

Johnny stepped out of his small apartment on Costin Avenue and unlocked the door to his car. As he sat down on the leopard print driver's seat, his cell phone vibrated in his back pocket. He reached into his tight stretch jeans and pulled out the phone. It was Rick from Alcoholics Anonymous. "Sorry Rick, you're going to voicemail and I'm going to have a few beers," laughed Johnny as he started the engine.

It had been nearly three weeks since he had been to an AA meeting. Johnny thought that he was doing pretty well for himself nowadays. He was finally making enough money to pay for both his apartment and taking care of Janine, his girlfriend.

The last time Johnny had gotten kicked out of an apartment was sometime in April. He was a cocky punk rocker with supercharged spiked hair that didn't give a shit about anyone except his friends and his girlfriend. His battle with the bottle seemed never-ending; at times where Johnny thought that he could safely have a few drinks and nothing more, he ended up either passed out in front of whichever apartment he was living room or in the backseat of his car with Janine driving home.

Janine's patience for her boyfriend had sometimes worn thin. She threatened to leave him every time he fell off the wagon, which usually resulted in Johnny deterring into a realm of hardcore drinking.

The outside air was pouring into the vehicle as Johnny stepped on the gas pedal. Driving was one of his few passions in life; whenever he had gotten an eviction notice, the first thing he would do was hop in his Monte Carlo and drive until he was almost completely out of gas. He babied his car as much as he could. There was never a moment where the thing wasn't shiningly clean.

Johnny pulled up to a red light. Bobbing his head up and down to the sounds of The Clash, he took a sip out of a can of cherry cola that must have been sitting inside the car since the weekend. The nighttime air was getting cooler, it felt more like winter than late spring.

He was excited to be going over to Dez's apartment. Being a recipient of severe heartbreak himself over the years, he knew exactly what his best friend was going through. The only helpful aspects of those ages were partying, alcohol, friends and meaningless sex with women. He wanted to be there for Dez, and wanted to make him laugh like they used do in high school.

Johnny's heart felt a pang for Dez; he remembered the very first time seeing his friend and Koral together. It was almost a year ago around this time, he figured to himself. Walking into the crowded Chinese restaurant, Janine and he sat across from the couple. He distinctly could remember the sheer bliss in the eyes of both Dez and Koral. It was almost as if Johnny could feel the couple's love protrude from across a table filled with plates of crispy orange chicken and fried rice.

Driving back from that lunch, he sent Dez a text message that read: "She's awesome. I'm really happy for you two." I can't believe that was almost a year ago, thought Johnny. Although he and his best friend had drifted apart somewhat during the past year, it felt good to be an important part of Dez's life again.

Johnny drove past the diner that he and his friends had gone to almost every-day in high school. Chester's house wasn't too far away from here. Rounding the corner after the greenhouse, it was the small blue house on the left side of the road.

He gave two honks of the horn as he pulled into Chester's driveway. Johnny reached into the CD holder on the car visor and grabbed the mix of '80s metal bands that Janine had burned for him a few weeks ago.

A shadowy figure erupted from beneath the large oak tree in front of the house. Chester was wearing his dark brown Stetson cowboy hat and a bright orange t-shirt that read "Vince For Governor."

Chester opened the Monte Carlo door and plumped down into the passenger side seat. "You're listening to Poison, good choice Johnny," said Chester as he gave his friend a high five. "So, are we looking at a typical night here? Or is Dez going to give us a nice, big smile?" he asked.

"I really don't know. You know how he's been recently, I'll be surprised if he only spends half the time talking about Koral," said Johnny.

Chester frowned and rolled up the window. "I really wish that kid would take a step back and realize that life has to move on. He can't be sitting in that apart-ment everyday, wasting away and being depressed."

"What do you want me to do, dude?" Johnny was now focusing on the road, and reached for the radio dial to turn down the volume. "When you're in a rela-tionship with someone whom you think is "the one" and it ends abruptly, it's going to take its toll whether we like it or not."

"That's true," said Chester. "I just worry about him a lot. I miss the Dez that would go out with us, get drunk and end up fighting a random jock at a bar in Boston. Koral was a really cool chick, I'll admit, but she ripped his poor heart out."

Ratt's "Round and Round" was playing in the background. Johnny flipped on his directional when the car rolled up to a red light. "I know, dude, I know. We're just going to have be there for him no matter what. He'll eventually get over it; it'll just take some time."

The traffic light turned green. Dez's house was around the next corner. Johnny pulled behind Dez's black Jeep in the driveway. As the two stepped out of the car and walked past their friend's car, Chester noticed a large black trash bag lodged in the backseat.

"Hey, do you think that's some of Koral's stuff?" asked Chester.

"It probably is, I wouldn't doubt it," replied Johnny as the two walked up the stairs to the second floor of the house.

Chester banged on the door and then tried to turn the handle. It was locked. "Dude, let us in!" he shouted.

Peeking through the window, Johnny could see Dez get up from the living room couch. With a bottle of Bud Light in his hand, he walked over to the door and unlocked it.

"Hey guys, what's up?" asked Dez as he opened the door. He was wearing stressed jeans and a plain black t-shirt. His hair was tied back into a white bandanna.

Johnny and Chester walked into the house. Chester sat down at the kitchen table to fumble through a *Guitar Monthly* magazine.

"Beer, anyone?" asked Dez. Both Johnny and Chester grunted in approval, and Dez tossed two bottles at them. He grabbed another one for himself and twisted off the cap.

What a scene, thought Dez. Looking at his two best friends sipping beer and peering at a guitar magazine sent a shockwave of normalcy through his mind. He could remember sitting in this same kitchen after a trip to see Koral, with his suitcase and carry-on bag thrown to the floor. Chester was usually the one waiting for him at the baggage claim. His friend had always given him a hug as soon as Dez appeared out of the terminal.

Last summer was his first trip out to see Koral. The plane ride there was nerve-racking. There wasn't a feeling of nervousness in his body, it was only a sense of apprehension; he missed his girlfriend.

Dez was snapped out of his daydream when Johnny poked him in the side. "You alright?" asked the tight-shirted Johnny.

"Yeah, I'll be fine man. I'll be fine," replied Dez as he stared off into space. He quickly retorted back into a stream of consciousness. "Nathan should be home soon. He was working until 6 but he probably went to see his girlfriend right after. I left him a message saying that you guys would be here."

"Good, I miss that little fucker," said Chester as he flipped through the remaining pages of the magazine.

Johnny wandered into the living room and sat down on the couch. He grabbed the remote and began to flip through the stations. "What channel is the

Sox game on? I can't find it!" he shouted from his laid-back position on the couch.

"Channel 51!" screamed Chester and Dez from the kitchen.

"So dude, how are you? You need to talk about anything?" asked Chester as he put down the magazine with a concerned look on his face. He took a sip of his beer and looked directly at Dez.

"Tomorrow is the one-year anniversary of her coming up here for the first time. It's killing me, Chester," replied Dez as he threw the bottle cap he'd been playing with across the kitchen and into the barrel. "I really don't know what to do here. I wake up every fucking morning and I think of her. I walk into the bathroom to take a shower and I think of her. I'm finding small things in my room that she either gave me or left here. I can't get away from this painful feeling inside of me."

It was sometimes hard to describe the feeling that Dez was talking about. It was a sensation that felt vacant and lonely in a way, but at the same time bursting with heated belligerence and unabashed anger. Dez's chest started to breathe more heavily as he looked down at the table.

"I know it hurts bro, but it's something you have to go through," Chester said. His attention was now fully focused on his friend. "The one-year thing must be killing you on the inside, and for that, I feel for you. I'm not going to lie; the next month, two months, whatever it's going to be, it's going to be very, *very* hard on your body, mind and your heart. Just remember that I'm here for you."

Johnny let out a behemoth belch from the living room. Chester laughed. "And you have that asshole in there," he said, smiling.

Dez forced a smile, which quickly turned into the signature frown that had been stuck on his face for the last two months. He appreciated the kind words from Chester, but deep down inside he knew that nothing was going to mend his heartbreak.

"Guys, the Sox are winning," said Johnny as tossed his empty bottle into the sink. He opened the refrigerator door and grabbed another one. "Millar hit a shot that cleared the Green Monster, they're up by two now."

Chester cheered and headed into the living room. He sat down on the left side of the couch and placed his feet on the coffee table in front of him, which was strewn with newspapers, CDs, an empty glass and a deck of cards. "These guys better win tonight, they're already two and a half games behind the goddamn Yankees," he said maliciously while glaring at the television screen.

Dez set his beer down on the coffee table and headed to the bathroom. He closed the door behind him, took a deep breath and looked at himself in the mirror. Toughen up, he thought to himself. "These guys are here for you, let them cheer you up. They're your best friends, Dez," he whispered to himself.

He flushed the toilet and opened the bathroom door. As he walked into the kitchen, he heard a car pull up in the driveway. He leaned over the sink and looked out the window through the drapes. The overbearingly loud muffler noise signaled only one car that Dez knew of: Nathan's black 1989 Mustang.

Nathan had been driving with Dez late last year when they had passed a house with the Mustang in front. The "For Sale" sign on the front made Nathan's eyes light up as he forced Dez to pull an illegal u-turn in the middle of the road.

The car had given Dez's brother nothing but problems over the past few months. First, Nathan took it to a mechanic to fix the brake pads. A thousand dollars later, he found out that it also needed a new fan-belt and an engine over-haul.

It really didn't matter to Nathan. He loved the thing, and there was nothing that was going to stop him from driving it around like it was a 10,000 pound bar of 24-karat gold on wheels.

Dez had already joined the other two in the living room when his brother had come through the door. Chester and Johnny jumped up and gave Nathan high fives and playful shoves, yelling at him to hang out with them more often.

"You little bastard, every time we come by here you're either out with your chick or at work," jokingly commented Johnny. "I think it's time for you to spend more time with your two adopted older brothers."

Nathan laughed and placed his keys on the living room coffee table. "Hey, I missed you guys too," he said with a large grin on his face.

Schilling throws his eighth strikeout of the night as the Sox exit the seventh inning with a 3-1 lead. Nathan reached for the television remote and turned the volume up. "Looks like the Sox are having a good night," he said.

Dez played with his bandanna and turned to Nathan. "Where did you go after work?" he asked.

"I went to see Lauren at work for a bit. We got something to eat during her break," Nathan replied. He went into his room and changed into a pair of Nike shorts.

Chester stood up and stretched. He looked at his messenger bag on the living room floor. It was about time that the "itch" has encompassed his body. "I'll be right back, guys," he said as he picked up the bag and headed into the bathroom.

"I'd sit him down and have a serious talk about doing that shit if I didn't have addictions of my own," Johnny thought aloud. He winked at Nathan, and Dez smiled.

"See? There's that smile that we all miss, brother!" said Johnny excitingly as he jumped out of his seat. "Just think dude, pretty soon we'll all be at bar, minus your little bro since he's a baby, and you'll be able to pick up chicks based on the natural fact that they all love your hair."

Nathan punched Johnny in the arm and laughed. Dez smiled again, although to him it felt somewhat forced. "I know, dude. I just need time to let all of this heal before I can be myself again," he said while looking at the ceiling. "I keep telling myself that this happened for a reason, and although I haven't figured out that reason just quite yet, it'll come to me eventually."

The words coming out of his mouth felt like cliché advice that almost everyone had given him. At times, Dez had believed what he just said. *It happened for a reason. Everything happens for a reason.*

Dez sighed and differentiated his attention to both the night sky shining into the apartment and the Red Sox game on television.

Look at that! Manny Ramirez hits his 17th homer of the year as the Sox continue to dominate this game. Whoa boy, that was a rocket shot! Chester shouted, "That's fucking awesome!" from the bathroom. He had snorted a full line of crystal meth and then sat on the toilet seat cover to collect himself. He threw some water on his face and made his way back to the gang. He knew that the rest of them did not care about his habit, but he still felt fairly embarrassed every time he hung out with them being completely strung out on crank.

Chester rejoined the group in the living room and sat down next to Nathan, who looked like he was about to pass out and fall asleep in front of everyone. Chester nudged him and he jumped up. "I'm awake guys, I'm awake," Nathan said.

"If you're tired kiddo, go to bed, we won't be too loud out here," said Dez, who for some reason felt tired himself. It wasn't necessarily a long day for him, however, his strength had dwindled since the mid-afternoon panic attack.

"Not a bad deal. Bed time for me, I guess," said Nathan. He checked his cell phone for any messages and walked into the kitchen. Minutes later he returned and said his goodbyes to the group, who were completely fixated on the remaining innings of the Red Sox game.

"I'm officially off to bed now guys," Nathan said as he rubbed his eyes. "Let's all do something this weekend."

Chester looked up from the television. "Sounds good kid, you better fucking be around or you're going to upset us all!" he said with a hearty laugh. Johnny gave Nathan a little wave, and Dez continued to stare at the television screen.

Nathan walked into his room and closed the door. Dez got up from the couch and headed into the kitchen. "Anybody want anything?" he asked as he washed his hands in the sink. Johnny grunted for another drink and Chester remained silent.

Both were fixated on the baseball game. *Going into the top of the ninth inning, the Sox hold a three-run lead over the Orioles. Keith Foulke is coming in to close and hopefully wrap up another win for Boston.* Johnny looked over at Dez, who was now standing next to the living room window.

I wonder what she's doing right now, Dez thought to himself. He sighed, looked back at his friends and joined them on the couch. "Nice to see the Sox winning," he commented. "What are you guys up for this weekend?"

Chester turned his attention away from the game. "Hmmm…good question," he pondered. He scratched his chin and adjusted his cowboy hat in his reflection in the television screen. "I'm working a double shift on Friday, but Saturday we could either hang out here again or hit up Vincenzo's."

Johnny considered the question and rolled his eyes. "Whatever we do, I'm sure it'll involve some drinking," he said with a sly smile.

Dez took a breath and looked outside again. *Foulke throws three consecutive strikeouts as the Sox will take this one, 4-1.* Johnny let out a small cheer and stood up. "Well, let's hope the Yankees lost tonight," he said. "If we sweep this series with Baltimore we'll have a good chance of being in first place again."

Chester picked up the remote and changed the channel. "I can't stand the after-game show on that channel," he said while gulping the remaining slurps of his beer. Johnny yawned and reached into his jacket pocket for a tube of lip balm.

"Well, I think I'm ready for some sleep," he said with another yawn. "Chester dude, you all set?"

Chester stretched his back and readjusted his cowboy hat. He looked over at Dez and then back at Johnny. "Sure, Dez looks like he's ready to pass out himself, let's go," he said.

Johnny unhinged his keychain from his white studded belt and walked towards the front door. Chester gave Dez a small hug and smiled. "Cheer up a bit bro," he said casually while digging for his cell phone in his front jeans pocket. "We'll go out this weekend and have a good time, I promise."

Dez forced out a small grin and shook his head. "Thanks for everything dude. You know I appreciate it," he said. His grin had now turned into nearly a full smile. "Let me walk you guys out."

He followed Chester to the front door, where Johnny was checking his voice-mail. Dez gave them each a high five and told them he'd call them both tomorrow.

Dez locked up the door as the two left and rested his forehead on it as he closed his eyes. The wooden door felt cold on his skin. He was alone again. Although he was silently wishing for his friends to leave the entire evening, there was a part of his mind that needed human contact to stay prominent. Dez had come to the realization that the empty pain smoldering inside of his chest was a constant; it'd be there whether he was with people or not.

He made his way over the bathroom but left the door open. He reached for his toothbrush and turned the cold water on in the sink. He stared at himself in the mirror while brushing his teeth. After washing his face, Dez untied his bandanna and threw it on the bathroom floor.

Walking into his bedroom, the sense of fatigue had mysteriously worn off. Even though he wasn't a fan of downing an anti-depressant to help relax his body, right now Dez would murder for even half a dose.

Stripping down to his black Calvin Klein briefs and a worn out white t-shirt, he slowly eased himself into his bed. Lying on his back, he turned his head to the left. A gigantic U2 poster from their 2001 Elevation Tour greeted him from the wall. Dez started to hum "I Will Follow" but stopped after a few seconds.

He turned his head to the right. Looking out his bedroom window, he could clearly see the night sky through a few branches of a nearby tree. There had been so many times where Koral would be curled up with him and he'd awake in the middle of the night to find her smiling. He missed that.

Dez could remember the way her teeth would chatter in the middle of the night. Although he continually joked around with her about it, he had secretly found it to be a cute quality in his then-girlfriend. Another flood of memories began to swathe his mind. He thought of having his legs entwined with hers, with her head gently rested on his chest as he kept his arms around her.

He wondered if she was sleeping next to her dog like she had always done. He wondered if she was thinking about right now. Most of all, he wondered if Koral had even missed him at all.

Dez continued to stare into the black sky.

CHAPTER 3

▼

"Morning, sweetie," she said with a faint smile. Her red hair was glistening in the sunlight pouring in from the window.

She leaned over and gave Dez a lengthy kiss, throwing her hands around his messed-up hair. He slowly placed his hands on her back, reaching down until he had a firm grip on her heart-shaped buttocks.

Dez could feel her hands pulling his body closer to her. With a quick motion, she pushed him down into the bed and straddled him. She leaned back and let her hair fall past her shoulders. Her pale body caroused Dez as his eyes rolled back with delight.

He reached up to caress her breasts as she gyrated in a back and forth motion. She leaned down to kiss him. "I love you so much baby," she said.

Dez wanted to reply but couldn't. Words weren't coming out of his mouth. Suddenly, he couldn't feel her on top of him anymore.

Dez opened his eyes and felt sweat pouring from his forehead. His arms jerked upward and he sat up. It was another dream. Cold air was making its way through the open window in his bedroom.

It's not fucking fair, he thought. These dreams were never-ending. Even if he went to sleep with a small sense of joy, it soon faded away in the dream world. The dominion of the unconscious was not kind to Dez.

Dez reached for the bottle of water at the side of his bed. Taking gigantic gulps, he closed his eyes and finished off the bottle. He tossed it against the wall and put his head on the pillow. Gripping the edge of the pillowcase, he fought back the feelings of the dream while looking outside.

Dez looked over at the clock. It was almost 4 a.m. It was going to be hard to fall back asleep. Even so, the threat of another ghost from the past lingered in the forefront. He didn't know if he could handle another one. It was bad enough dealing with everything while awake; facing his repulsive mindset alone in a dream was a fate far worse.

He wondered to himself. When will these dreams stop? Will they ever? How the hell am I going to deal with this everyday?

Questions danced in his mind as the moonlight started to fade away outside. He tossed and turned for a few minutes; there wasn't a comfortable spot anywhere in the bed. The sheets were scattered halfway on the bed, halfway on the floor. Dez pulled on the black and grey quilted blanket as he turned over onto his belly.

He could hear a police siren passing by outside. Although it felt like forever, his eyes gradually closed as he drifted back into a soft slumber.

*   *   *   *

Nathan poured milk into his cereal bowl. He hated working the morning shift at the grocery store. Even though he went to bed fairly early the night before after hanging out with his brother and his friends, he was still tired.

Heaping large spoonfuls of cereal into his mouth, he picked up the bowl and walked into the living room. He grabbed the remote from the coffee table and turned on the television.

Nathan flipped through the stations. He caught the last 30 seconds of highlights from last night's Red Sox game on "Sports Center" and then promptly changed the channel. He paused at CNN to catch the score of the Yankees game. The broadcast reporter was talking about something to do with planet alignments, but Nathan wasn't paying attention.

After finding out that the Yankees lost, he changed the channel again. He heard Dez's bedroom door creak open in the background. Still rubbing the sleep out of his eyes, Dez walked into the kitchen and opened the fridge.

"Hey Dez," Nathan casually remarked as he finished off the remaining bundles of cereal in the bowl.

Dez didn't hear his brother. His head was inside of the fridge, shoving beer bottles to the side as he groped for the container of orange juice, only to find that there was none left. "Fuck," he said as slammed the door shut.

He ventured into the living room and sat next to Nathan. Dez let out a sarcastic smile and threw his head back on the headrest of the couch. "Work soon?" he asked Nathan while putting a hand through his hair.

"Unfortunately, yes," answered his brother, who was engrossed in something that was on MTV. "I'm leaving here in 20 minutes."

Dez went back into his bedroom and closed the door behind him. He could feel it working within his stomach and traveling into his veins. Before long, it was in his chest. From here, the tears started to congeal behind his eyes as they started to escape.

With the salty discharge erupting from his eyes, all he could think in his mind was being with Koral exactly one year ago today. He threw his head into his hands and let the tears flow, leaving a wet mess on his palms.

Dez remembered sitting in his room with her after picking her up at the airport. She looked beautiful, he recalled. All the two could do was stare at each other. There was no outside world, according to the couple, that entire week. Her green eyes radiated with a sense of solitude that made Dez feel warm inside.

He remembered sitting on the living room couch, flipping through channels, with Koral in his arms, waiting for Johnny to call so he and Janine could meet Koral. *Let it go, Dez.* A voice in the back of his mind obtruded from the memoria, sounding stern and evil. *You don't need her, Dez.* It was getting louder.

Dez couldn't help himself. He thought of her hugging the blue teddy bear she had given him months before she flew up for the first time. It ripped him open inside as the tears became heavier and more recurrent.

His mind drifted into the memories: holding her hand while driving, giving her kiss at every red light, pulling up to his parents' house to introduce her. Every solitary moment of her visit was like an individual dagger piercing the open air as it ripped through his heart.

The harsh voice became more demanding. *Everything happens for a reason, Dez. Just let it go.* He tried to ignore it and allowed the memorial torture to continue.

Dez flashed back to waking up next to Koral for the first time. Her legs entwined with his, she gave him a soft kiss as he asked her how she slept. "I slept awesome. I love you," she replied with an ear-to-ear smile.

"One fucking year ago today," he said aloud to his empty room. His eyes itched from crying. The throbbing in his chest was still perceptible, there was no escaping it. The voice was starting to decay in the back of his mind. *You'll be fine, Dez. Move on. Everything happens for a reason.* Pretty soon, it had completely faded away.

Dez wiped his eyes and tried to collect himself. This entire day is going to kill me, he thought. He lied down on the bed. Staring at the ceiling, all that had encompassed his mind was her voice.

*   *   *   *

What seemed like hours had passed by. He must have fallen asleep, Dez thought. He reached over for his cell phone on the nightstand. It was a little past noon.

He forced himself out of bed and onto his feet. As he stretched, he noticed a small tear in the bottom of his white t-shirt. Dez ignored the hole and walked out of his bedroom and into the kitchen.

Dez was barely into the afternoon of the day, and already it had felt like he'd been awake for hours. He was determined to not let the day's implication destroy him at the brim of insanity; he was going to toughen up his image and attempt to enjoy the Friday. After all, his friends would be around later, and maybe with a little alcohol his mood would even out.

The sun was gleaming through the living room window. Dez opened the front door and peeked into the mailbox. Inside, he found this month's edition of *Maxim*, a bill from the cell phone company and a handwritten envelope addressed to both Nathan and him. It was probably a check from their Dad, he thought.

He stepped back into the apartment and dropped the mail on the kitchen table. Dez picked up the copy of *Maxim* and began to thumb through the pages. As he turned to the section on sex tips, a small wave of barrenness gripped his body and he tossed the magazine down. He flashed back to jokingly cutting out a section of the magazine last summer that included "Tips On Giving Your Boy-friend The Best Lap Dance He's Ever Had," which he had mailed to Koral a week before he made a trip out there to see her.

I'm going to be doing this all day today, Dez thought. He fought the urge to reminisce and made his way into the living room. The only thing that was keep-ing his mind somewhat intact was the glistening sunlight protruding through the windows of his apartment. Dez had believed for years that he suffered from Sea-sonal Affective Disorder, as he would fight dismal sentiments during the long winter months. Even knowing that he had Koral last winter, it was still tough for him to appreciate a buoyant mood.

Dez plopped down onto the brown armchair that graced the left side of the living room. He popped the recliner back and tilted his head to the side. The television wasn't on; he was left alone with nothing but the sunlight and his thoughts.

Dez looked over to the coffee table. He noticed a black marking on a corner of the glass coffee table in the center of the room. He flipped the recliner back into its normal position and walked over to inspect the marking.

Chester had written "BALLS" with a black magic marker. Dez let a smile overcome his face and shook his head. Chester had a knack for doing small things like that to get Nathan and him to laugh. He sat up and got out of the armchair.

Dez walked into the kitchen and reached for the handwritten envelope that was left in his mailbox. The front read, "To Dez and Nathan." He opened it and pulled a piece of thick beige paper that was folded into three sections overlapped over each other.

As he had believed, a check from his father slid out and fell onto the kitchen table. The check was made out for two hundred dollars, with a note that read "For my two sons."

"Big Jake," as many people had called him, tried his best to remain as close to his sons as possible after Dez and Nathan moved out of the house. It seemed like he never saw his children that often. Even though there were the occasional Sunday afternoon New England Patriots games and a few Red Sox games every once in a while, he missed his two sons.

Nathan had made more of a conscientious effort to see his father. He stopped by after work a few nights a week, since the house was a few streets over from the grocery store. He would always give Big Jake a high five and a hug after walking through the door.

Dez was always a topic of discussion during Nathan's short visits to their parents' house. "Are you sure he's doing okay?" his mother would continually ask him while sitting at their kitchen table. Nathan would assure Joanna that her son was fine, and just needed some time to be alone.

"I always loved that Koral. She was such a sweet girl," Joanna would frequently say.

Dez signed the back of the check and folded it in half. He grabbed a magnet from the fridge and stuck it there for his brother to see when he got home. The two hundred bucks would probably have to go to rent, thought Dez.

He was thinking of skipping a jog today and just making a run for a few errands. Dez turned on the shower in the bathroom and undressed. After showering, he headed into his bedroom and turned on the stereo.

The sounds of the new Morrissey record drowned out the outside world for Dez. He changed into jeans and a black t-shirt and sat on his bed. *And I'm not sorry, for the things I've done,* sang Morrissey. *I'm not looking, for just anyone.* The voluminous guitars and ever-haunting melodies eased Dez's mind into a realm of elation. *On competing, when will this tired heart stop beating?*

For a short while, the tribulations of his life subsided. Koral was nowhere to be found in his thoughts. Money issues, unemployment, family problems, they all drifted away while Dez was lost in the music. *It's all a game, existence is just a game.*

He's right, Dez thought. Existence is just a game; a game in which Dez was losing.

CHAPTER 4

▼

"It really comes down to the question of whether or not the diametric arguments of the parapsychologists' can be considered true," Professor Bruce Ulrich announced to his class. "Is death really the end of our existence as human beings?"

Professor Ulrich reached into his pockets and fumbled with the three quarters and two nickels at the bottom. "After all, the study of the "invisible" is an empire of science that no single scholar on this planet might be capable of. For over a century, scientists have claimed that our bodies survive the physical death, however, the mind can continue to live on."

He looked over at a student sitting in the front row of the classroom. "The realm of spiritualism has no place in science, right? If so, then why are scientists all over the globe *still* struggling with the ideas of survival after death?"

"Think about it. I'll see you guys on Monday. Remember, I want to know what you're doing for your end-of-summer-semester term papers."

The 23 students filed out of the Northern Boston University classroom while Professor Ulrich gathered his lecture notes. He placed them in a manila folder and stuck them in his aging, brown leather briefcase.

Even though it was close to 75 degrees outside, he decided to wear his favorite black suit jacket. Sure, he was wearing a Joy Division shirt underneath, which could be considered far from "professionalism" at a semi-prestigious university such as the one he was teaching, but he didn't care.

The first summer session of classes was beginning to wind down. Professor Ulrich always enjoyed teaching summer class at NBU. It wasn't like a normal semester; everything was so much more relaxed, including the lectures, which allowed for an increased curiosity in students eager to register for his classes.

He reached for his cell phone in the front pocket of the briefcase. One missed call and one voicemail. They were both from his ex-wife. Professor Ulrich sighed and draped the strap of his briefcase over his right shoulder.

He reached into his hair and pulled down the black sunglasses which had kept his bangs out of his face. He knew that he didn't look like the typical college professor; perhaps this was why there were so many female students asking him out for drinks after every class. Professor Ulrich chuckled and continued the walk back to his office.

He passed by a group of students lounging on the staircase in front of The Butterfield Building, which housed mostly faculty offices and the Dean of Students' office. The professor noticed Adam, one of his students from a psychology class he had taught during the spring semester. Adam walked up to him and smiled.

"Hey Professor, I just wanted to say thanks for giving me that 'A' in pysch class last semester," he proclaimed with a large grin on his face.

"Don't say thanks, kid, you *earned* that grade," Professor Ulrich said with a stern look. "Adam, students like you make it easier for me to teach at a university like this. You put the work in, and you got the grade you deserved."

Adam's smile grew, as well as his momentary ego. "Well, if I can't say thanks for giving me the grade, at least let me thank you for being such a cool professor," he said.

Professor Ulrich laughed and patted Adam on the back. "Keep up the good work, Adam. I'm in a little bit of a rush," he said after glancing at his watch. "Drop me a line through email if you need anything over the summer."

"Sure thing, take care professor," Adam said as he walked back down the stairs to his group of fellow students.

The professor headed into the building and into the lobby. He realized that it was students like Adam that made it a joy to teach at NBU. He pushed the up button in between the two elevators in front of him and looked at his watch again. There was a reason why she called, he thought to himself as the left elevator rang when it approached the lobby floor.

He stepped into the elevator and pressed the button for the fourth floor. Although he and Faith had divorced well over five months ago, she still attempted to look to him for consistent advice on everything from handling the rent for her apartment to figuring out how to work the digital cable in her living room.

Professor Ulrich was in a state of wonderment. "What can that woman possibly want this time?" he asked himself aloud in the empty elevator.

The elevator hit the fourth floor and the professor stepped out. His office was the third one in the right corridor. He walked past two of his fellow professors' offices. It looked as if Professor Griffin had decided to throw a private party by himself, as the man's office was littered with empty plastic cups and a large pizza box that was strewn across the desk amongst a mess of papers. That guy's alcoholism is really going to catch up with him someday, Professor Ulrich thought to himself as he ended his momentary peek into the office.

He didn't bother to look at Professor Levin's office. She was a 31-year-old prude, according the rest of the faculty in Professor Ulrich's department. Sure, she was hot, the professor thought to himself, but, there was no way in hell he was going get in her pants.

While unlocking the door to his office, the professor glanced over at her office for a quick second. Professor Levin was fixated on something on her computer screen, and there was maybe half an inch of cleavage showing as she leaned over to inspect whatever she was reading.

Professor Ulrich walked into his office after attempting to ignore his co-worker's breasts and flung his keys on the sturdy pine desk in the corner. He flipped the light switch on the wall even though there was enough sunlight pouring into the room to see clearly.

The professor turned his computer on and turned to the mini-refrigerator behind him. He pulled out an energy drink and opened it. After taking a swig from the small blue and silver can, he sat down and pulled out his cell phone from the briefcase.

"Hi Bruce, it's Faith. Listen, I know this is last minute, but I, I…don't know how to ask you this. Well, what I want is…well, um, listen, if you can come over for dinner either tonight or tomorrow night I'd, I'd, you know, really appreciate it. I know you're doing a lot of research and you're teaching a few classes, but I need to talk to you. Call me back, Bruce. Thanks, bye," her voicemail said.

Professor Ulrich cringed with anger. He finished chugging the energy drink, crunched the can in his left hand and threw it against the wall. That fucking bitch, he thought, she can't make up her goddamn mind.

He had been married to Faith for almost three years. The professor had met her at a bookstore in Cambridge nearly five years ago. He had noticed her looking at books on psychology while he was trying to find good texts to base a night class syllabus on.

That moment seemed just like yesterday, thought the professor. Faith was wearing tight black stretch pants, a pink studded belt and a white blouse. Her blonde hair had a few black streaks in it, and Professor Ulrich remembered that he was instantly attracted to her.

He casually struck up a conversation with her and the two made plans to meet for drinks that upcoming weekend. Faith was only a few years younger than him, and it was easy for the two to connect immediately.

Professor Ulrich was only 36 years old at the time and had never been married. Besides two long-term relationships, one that had just recently ended a few months before he had met Faith, he had spent the majority of his time on his scientific work and not his romantic life. In the grand scheme of life, he would say, it is always best to never let another human being drag you down with the temptations of sex, companionship and…love.

Love was a fanatical feeling for the professor. Faith brought out all the best in him, whether it was teaching a college class, writing landmark articles in peer-reviewed science journals, or just merely being a better man.

He had fallen head first in love with her, and vice versa for Faith. After six months of dating, the professor asked her to move in with him. He had kept a good deal on a swanky two-bedroom place on Commonwealth Ave., since it was easy for him to commute using the subway. Faith was working at law firm in downtown Boston, so it all made perfect sense.

Life was going well for Professor Ulrich at the time. He was enjoying teaching a Northern Boston University, and he had a gorgeous woman in his life that made him extremely happy.

It only took him three months to work up the nerve to propose to Faith. He even came up with the perfect way to do it. They both shared a love for U2, and he had scored tickets to all four of their shows in Boston the last time they toured.

During the last night of their four-night stand, Professor Ulrich pulled the one-karat princess cut diamond ring from his pocket, wrapped his arms around Faith, and asked her to marry him while the band was playing "Where The Streets Have No Name."

Already wrapped up within the sentiment of the song, with tears pouring down her cheek, Faith let out a faint "yes" and kissed the professor.

Now, whenever he heard that song, he wanted to smash someone's face with a baseball bat.

Professor Ulrich snapped out of the reminiscing trip and refocused himself on the computer in front of him. He had 33 unread emails, mostly from students either questioning their spring semester grades or from faculty members asking him help cover some of their bare summer classes. And of course, one was from Faith. The subject line was a simple "hi."

The professor winced and deleted it. Ever since the divorce, Faith would not let him go, even though she was the one to kick-start the separation process. It almost seemed trivial to Professor Ulrich; he honestly believed Faith to be unlike any other woman he had spent time with. For most of their five-year relationship, she wowed him with her uncanny ability to make him smile from ear to ear with romantic and harmonious delight.

It was only during the final months that chaos was invited into their personal space. Faith had revealed to him at various points throughout their time together that Professor Ulrich was one of the only guys that she truly had fallen in love with.

She had a history of abuse from multiple partners when she was in her 20s, and ended up falling for a guy who had her fooled as a genuine individual who actually cared about her. Faith wound up engaged to him, and it ended with her having four broken ribs and a fractured nose after a lengthy argument.

Ever since then, Faith had trouble staying with someone whom she truly had feelings for, including the professor. Her uncertainty had nearly faded away when the engagement approached, however, it was only after the ring was on her finger that Professor Ulrich had noticed an anomalous change in her mood in daily life.

Faith would draw herself away from the professor, both emotionally and sexually, to the point of eruption. She used the word "stress" way too much for his comfort and sanity, and proclaimed it to be the reason why she was withdrawing from him. While it was true that Professor Ulrich had sometimes become so emaciated within his work that he would become easily irritated with some of Faith's quirks, it was nowhere near the line of pushing for a split between the two.

It was a cool spring evening when the fuel for Faith's fire had finally resulted in a relational detonation. Professor Ulrich had come home late from an afternoon class at NBU, already frazzled from dealing with an uninterested class for three hours, and was looking forward to sitting down to dinner with Faith and going over wedding plans.

She seemed completely disinterested in making any progress, and the professor made sure that he voiced the concern. Faith blew up at him and had told him that she "wasn't sure whether or not her heart was in this completely."

After 20 minutes of screaming at each other, the professor told her to leave the apartment. It took the two almost a week to resolve the problem, and upon the promise to stay true to each other, all wedding plans were furthered and they had set a date.

The wedding ceremony itself was small. The professor joked around for a month leading up to the actual wedding, stating that his dream ceremony would look just like the one held in Guns 'N' Roses' video for "November Rain."

Professor Ulrich invited his best friend Keith to be his best man, and Faith had asked her older sister to stand in as maid of honor. They were married in a public garden near the professor's apartment, and held a small reception at a function hall down the street from Faith's old apartment in the suburbs.

It only took a year and a half of marriage to lead to dissolution. What a fucked up year, thought Professor Ulrich.

The phone at his desk rang. "Dr. Ulrich here," he answered.

"Hey Professor, it's Dane. I found some of those documents you were looking for," said Dane, one of the professor's graduate assistants in the science department offices. He sounded a little out of breath and overly jubilant. "You're never going to believe what I found."

"Interesting. Are you at the lab right now?" said Professor Ulrich.

"No, I'm at home. I have a few things that are absolutely insane. I had to sneak them out, so I just stuck them in my bag," Dane said in return. "I dropped by your office a few hours ago but you were probably in class."

"Yeah, I had a class. Listen, I'll drop by your house in an hour or two," said the professor.

"Awesome, take care Professor," Dane said before hanging up the phone.

The professor smiled and hung up the phone. His new side project was something that had him jittery and animated.

Although Professor Ulrich was mostly schooled in the psychological sciences, including neuropsychology and parapsychology, he took an interest in almost anything scientific that was going on in the world news.

The professor taught a course a couple years ago in astronomy, even though he did not have the proper accreditation to head such a class. NBU was going through a period in which the percentage of incoming freshmen was steadily decreasing each year, causing the university to refuse tenure to deserving professors.

Three colleagues of Professor Ulrich found themselves denied tenure, resulting in two of them finding employment at other colleges in Massachusetts, and the other heading to California. Thus came the Dean of Administration at NBU to approach professors to take on extra classes in their respective schedules.

The astronomy class was an appealing juncture for the professor; he found himself extremely intrigued by the skies and space. He would spend hours with Faith on the roof of their apartment complex gazing at the sky. As he could recall, she would fall asleep in his arms under a blanket while the professor would stare into the sky.

Ever since teaching the course, Professor Ulrich attempted to attend astronomy conventions across the country during the fall academic season, networking with others in the science fields to further his study of space.

While spending time in the mountains of New Hampshire during NBU's spring break in March, the professor glared into the night sky to see Venus making a brilliant appearance amongst the stars.

Professor Ulrich drove to a remote cabin owned by his cousin Charles near the White Mountains in New Hampshire on the Thursday night previous to spring break. He had canceled his classes on the Friday to get a head start on the long drive up there.

It would be the first time in a few years that Faith had not accompanied him on a vacation. The professor figured it would be best to spend the time alone with nothing but a few bottles of wine and the mid-term exams for all of his classes that needed to be graded.

Taking an interest in Venus' trek across the sky, he conducted a small photo exhibit with NBU's astronomy department upon the a few weeks after returning from spring break. After discussing the planet's trek with a fellow professor in the science department, he was informed that in the middle of June, Venus would cross the face of the sun in a near-perfect alignment with Earth for a short period.

This alignment and trek across the sun at what astronomers called inferior junction was scheduled to take place on June 15. Professor Ulrich had thought about inviting interested students to the university to watch the exposure, however, he figured that some of NBU's deans would have a problem with students staying overnight at one of the university's science labs.

The professor had some additional time on his hands after the spring semester had ended, and after setting up a summer schedule of classes at the university, he decided to tackle a full report on the Venus transit in hopes of publishing it for one of several potential science journals.

He had asked Dane, a work study assistant, to help him research the last time such a transit occurred, which was in 1882. The professor was excited to see what Dane had unearthed. He quickly checked some of his stocks on the web, browsed a few different websites to find Red Sox tickets, and then decided to close down shop for the day.

Professor Ulrich locked up his office and made his way to the elevator. After pressing the down button, he readjusted the strap on his bag and placed his cell phone in his left suit jacket pocket. I'm not going to call her back, he thought.

After all, he could picture the scenario in his head. Faith would get drunk during dinner and cry uncontrollably, admitting to the professor that she had made a mistake. Professor Ulrich had more common sense than she could have imagined; he was not going to succumb to mind games that people their age shouldn't be playing with each other.

He stepped into the elevator and looked at his watch. It was almost five, and he was hoping that he'd be able to squeeze a jog in after meeting up with Dane. A rush of enthusiasm overcame the professor's body as he thought of the possibilities of what the graduate assistant had discovered. Dane never gets excited about anything, he thought, so he must have found something that the professor would truly enjoy.

Professor Ulrich stepped out of the elevator when it reached the building's lobby and casually scooted down the staircase after passing through the front doors. He waved to a few students sitting around a tree near the Butterfield Building and headed over to the parking lot.

The professor's black 2001 Lexus hadn't been cleaned in months. Various papers were strewn across the backseat, along with multiple CDs, textbooks and magazines. Professor Ulrich reached into his pocket for his car keys and unlocked the driver's side door. He sat down on the cushiony leather seat and tossed his bag beside him.

He fumbled in his jacket pocket for his cell phone and pulled it out. He flipped it open and scrolled down to Faith's number in the phonebook. Professor Ulrich hesitated for a moment and scratched his face. "Should I call her?" he asked himself aloud in the car.

The professor adjusted his rear view mirror and sighed. He flung the phone on the passenger's side seat and said, "Fuck it."

He had successfully resisted the urge to call his ex-wife and started the car's engine. He reached over to a pile of CDs sitting on the seat next to him and scanned through all of them. Professor Ulrich was in the mood for something angry and volatile. The Smiths weren't going to do it. Neither would The Cure or Aerosmith. He popped in an old Metallica album and revved the engine.

$$* \quad * \quad * \quad *$$

Dane paced back and forth in the living room of his small apartment. Grasping a large manila envelope, he stared nervously at the window. It had been over an hour, and still the professor had not arrived.

He sat down on the small red couch in the corner of the room and looked down at the envelope. He shuffled his short brown hair with his left hand and fixed the collar to his green button-down dress shirt.

Professor Ulrich is going to flip out when he sees this, he thought. The clerk at the public records library had continually checked on him while he was searching for the documents the professor had asked for. Dane could not believe that what he held in the envelope in his hand was buried in that public records library.

Dane was shaking nervously as he heard a car door slam in the driveway. He jumped out of his seat and ran to the door. Professor Ulrich had just reached down to turn the doorknob when Dane furiously opened it himself.

"Dane! What's wrong buddy?" the professor asked with a concerned look on his face.

"Professor, you're never going to believe this. Sit down and take a look at this." The words could barely escape Dane's mouth.

The professor looked at Dane with cautious eyes and smiled. "Wow, you must have some good news for me, kid."

Dane looked at up the gleaming professor and nodded his head. "Sit down," he said with a stern look on his face.

Professor Ulrich flashed a quick smile and sat down next to a pile of clothes on the couch. He crossed his legs and leaned back into the cushion. "Okay now, tell me what you've found, Dane."

Dane closed his eyes for a moment, then reopened them and looked away. "Before I tell you what's in this envelope, how does this whole Venus thing pan out?"

The professor uncrossed his legs and leaned forward. He gathered his thoughts. "Well, basically, Venus will be in a straight, near-perfect alignment with the sun and the earth for a short period of time on June 15. It's an east-to-west passage that will last just over six hours and 12 minutes."

Dane was now staring straight ahead. "Anything else?" His hands had finally stopped trembling.

Professor Ulrich cleared his throat and looked directly at Dane. "More than half the world will be able to see the rare event. Most of Europe and Asia will have the chance to witness it, as well as the eastern two-thirds of Africa. Some of South America will be able to see it, and there's a slanted line going down the middle of this country that cuts through somewhere in Montana and goes through Texas. Everyone living east of there will be able to see it." The professor cleared his throat again and glanced over at the manila envelope in Dane's hands. "Dane, is everything okay?"

Dane licked his lips and let out a small smile. "Professor, maybe I'm looking way too much into what I've found. I really don't know. Maybe it's my nerd-esque brain working on overdrive."

"Dane, just let me see what you've found. You've got me all riled up now." The professor was now beaming with delight.

Dane stood up and handed the envelope to the professor. "I'm going to tell you something right now. If that document is fake, I'm going to be bullshit at those bastards down at the public records library."

The professor patted Dane on the back and grinned. "Thanks for getting this for me, Dane. I knew it'd be hard to find a document from that long ago. I'm surprised you've even found anything at all."

"I suggest you go home and read that as soon as you can. I've had enough for one day," Dane said with a sense of apprehension in his voice.

Professor Ulrich was confused. There was obviously something wrong with the situation in front of him. "Dane, should I read this right now?"

Dane was now in the kitchen. He poked his head over from the counter and looked at the professor. "Call me tomorrow. I'm going to go to bed." He knew that if the professor read what was inside that envelope in front of him, neither of them would be able to sleep tonight. It was already apparent that he'd be up all night himself.

The professor's mind was running with both stimulation and intrigue. However, Dane's behavior was bothering him. He gave in and agreed to check out the document at home. "Ok kiddo, thanks again. I'll talk to you tomorrow, ok? Get some sleep, you looked absolutely spooked."

Dane nodded and walked the professor out the front door. Professor Ulrich turned and looked at him. He gave the young student a quick nod and pulled out his car keys after sliding the manila envelope under this right arm.

The professor opened the door to his car and heard the thud of Dane's apartment door slamming shut. He eased himself into the driver's seat and placed the envelope on the stack of CDs next to him. He stared at the envelope for a full couple minutes before starting the engine.

He backed out of the driveway and sped towards the highway. It was only a 20-minute ride home, plenty of time to drag out the excitement for what was contained in that envelope. The sounds of The Cure drowned out the outside air that was pouring in from the open two windows in the back of the car. The sunroof was open and the summer night sky allowed its moon to shine light inside of the vehicle.

The professor pulled off the highway and onto a street off of the exit. Pulling up to a red light, he glanced over at the envelope. There was something about the calmness of the evening in contrast to what lay inside the envelope. The curiosity was tearing away at the layers of his brain; his knuckles twitched while he grasped the steering wheel when the traffic light turned green.

Passing through the empty streets, Professor Ulrich let his mind drift into the tranquil world outside of his car. He had completely forgotten about Faith; the contents of that manila envelope were all he needed tonight. Visions of her blonde hair falling into her face as she cried faded into the vague unknown of the night.

His apartment was just around the corner. Luckily, there was a space nearly a block away from his residence. The professor parallel parked the car and shut off the engine. He grabbed for his brown leather messenger bag in the backseat and slid the envelope into its front pouch.

Walking for a few minutes, he looked up at the sky. It was a beautiful night, he thought. He wondered how amazing the Venus transit would look in a few days. It was something that the professor was looking forward to tremendously.

Professor Ulrich jogged up the stairs to his apartment complex. He pulled open the lobby doors and ran up the stairs. Normally, he'd catch an elevator because he was too lazy to walk the four floors to his apartment, but too much anticipation was carousing through his veins.

After unlocking the door to his apartment, he threw his keys on the desk to the left and turned on the kitchen and living room lights. Taking off his suit jacket, he removed his cell phone from the front pocket and placed it in his charger on the kitchen counter.

The professor made his way into the living room and sat down on the burgundy couch across from the television set. He took the manila envelope out of his bag and dropped it on the wooden coffee table in front of him. He walked over to window in the living room and pulled the shades open. After opening the window halfway to let the cool summer breeze in, the professor sat down on the couch again.

Professor Ulrich grabbed the envelope and unhinged the small metal piece at the top. Immediately, his nose picked up what smelled like old, rotten newspapers. Reaching into the envelope, he pulled out two thick pieces of paper that had handwriting on them.

He felt the texture of the papers; they felt exactly as he imagined 122-year-old papers would feel. The gritty edges, the overpowering tang of rotten dust; it all added to the exhilarating feeling burning inside of the professor.

The words jumped off the papers and into his eyes. Paragraph by paragraph, he could not believe what he was reading. The horror, the revulsion in front of him buried a sense of shock into his mind.

He turned to the second page, his hands vacillating with absolute fright and disgust. Visions of what he was interpreting danced around in his head, protruding a realm of dread throughout his entire body.

Professor Ulrich's eyes stared through the paper when he finished reading the text. He sat gaping into nothingness, his body filled with utter terror.

Outside, the night sky was beaming its moonlight into the silent apartment.

CHAPTER 5

▼

It is hard to explain the recent happenings in the town without presenting a realm of darkness and obsession. Upon the great eclipse in the skies came a horrific sight.

I could not believe my eyes at the events that occurred. Father was buying items for the house at a store at the town square while I was sitting on a bench outside. I usually enjoyed the sights of the area. It was not often that I accompanied my father into the town for his weekly errands. It was usually I who would stay back at the house with mother.

It was quite early in the morning; I could remember walking and holding father's hand and barely being able to walk because I was so tired. On his weekly trips into the town, Mr. Jenkins from across the way would often join us in our path. However, this morning, Mr. Jenkins was nowhere to be found.

The town square in Revmont was usually teeming with patrons from the area. This morning, however, it seemed as if many of the town's people decided to stay indoors. Upon our arrival, father asked me sit on the bench outside the general store while he went to talk to the shopkeeper.

After a few minutes, I heard a great yelp come from across the street. A man dressed in a torn suit stumbled towards the town square, limping along with one arm strayed towards the air in front of him. The other seemed stuck by his left side.

His face looked decayed and bloody, as if someone had attacked him with knives. What happened next will forever haunt my mind. A woman from the nearby tailor's shop approached the man in hopes of finding out what was wrong. With one quick motion, he grabbed for her neck and tore off a large piece of flesh, sending blood spurting everywhere.

I screamed and my father and the shopkeeper ran out of the store. Suddenly, it might have been twenty to thirty of these other monsters that resembled the first man who hobbled along the dirt road and began to attack the few patrons that were outside of the shops.

My father grabbed me by the hand and pulled me into the general store. He locked the door behind him. I saw Jensen, the shopkeeper, get swiped by one of the monsters. They pounced on him, bloody drool falling from their distorted mouths. Within minutes, a few of those things had ripped off his limbs and devoured them.

With tears in my eyes, I held on to my father's side as tight as I could. He stroked my hair and kept repeating, 'Hilda, it'll be alright." He boarded up the two windows and the only door to the store with pieces of lumber from the back room. I sat and stared at the floor.

Two hours had passed, and all we could hear were the screams of the monsters outside. Banging on the door of the store, they tried their best to break it down. I don't know how much longer the planks will last before they are successful.

I sit here now and write on the few pieces of paper I could find in the store. I fear that my 14 years on this planet will be my last. Father sits next to me with an axe he found in the back, waiting for the inevitable to occur.

I wish that this horrible ordeal will end, but my father insists that their numbers are growing. The banging of the ghouls does not end, and neither do their bloodcurdling groans.

I pray to God that he will bless us with the safety we need to survive.

Hilda Bentlon

CHAPTER 6

▼

Dez placed his hand on the 50-pound barbell and closed his eyes. With a heavy rush of adrenalin and anger, he lifted it until his bicep crunched. After a few repetitions, he let out a breath and picked it up with his other hand.

It had been a few weeks since Dez had last worked out. The thrill of weight-lifting vanished since Koral had left him. For a few weeks following the breakup, he didn't jog or partake in any type of exercise whatsoever.

With another breath, he curled the weighty barbell and let out a small sigh. Following the few repetitions, he dropped the barbell to the floor and sat down on the living room couch. His chest pulsating up and down, he breathed heavily and used his white t-shirt to wipe his brow.

Dez was glad that he had successfully made it through the previous day. He knew the one-year anniversary of Koral's first trip to Boston would take its toll on his already unhealed heart.

He shook the rush left in his body from the workout and stood up. His arms outstretched, he felt the burn in his arms. Good workout, he thought.

Dez walked over to the kitchen and reached into the refrigerator. Grabbing a bottle of water, he unscrewed the cap and chugged nearly half of it.

After taking a shower, he walked into his bedroom and fumbled through his closet. On the floor lay a black t-shirt with a large white star embedded on the front. He could remember how much he loved the shirt, and how much he avoided wearing it ever since Koral left him.

Putting on a pair of green-tinted jeans and black socks, Dez reached for his black leather belt with small metal studs on the exterior and tightened the buckle.

As much as he wanted to, he felt that wearing the star t-shirt would be an added scar to his body.

For a moment, Dez wanted to forget everything about his past. He wanted to forget Koral, forget everything about her and every tiny notion of their relationship. He reached down for the shirt and held it up in the air. With a few beams of sunlight streaming their way into his bedroom, he attempted to smile and stood up.

Dez allowed his mind to drift into nothingness as he pulled open the bottom of the shirt and eased it over his arms and head. The bottom edge fell just above his belt; it was always a perfect fit over his torso.

He walked over to the mirror on his bedroom wall and stared directly into its center. The corpulence of the white star in the center edged its way into Dez's mind. There was something about it that represented everything astounding in his life: being rock 'n' roll, not giving a shit about anyone besides the people that mattered, his love of music, his bond with Nathan, and most importantly, his will to succeed with the cards he was dealt with.

Dez forced his mind back into a relative consciousness. He wasn't over Koral by any means, and there was no way he was going to compel himself into believing otherwise. Still gazing into the mirror, his focus shifted off the star in the center of his black t-shirt and onto his face.

"Dez, you look so fucking worn out," he thought aloud to the empty room. He watched himself mouth the words in the mirror. His unshaven cheeks and chin presented a vision of slothfulness and misery.

He could picture Koral's blood red painted fingernails squeezing the side of his shirt. She would always cry right above the right side of the star whenever she had to leave Boston to go back home. It was almost an unpatented ritual: Dez would always throw his favorite shirt on the last day of her trips.

In his mind, Koral was burying her pale white face into his chest, leaving small blue smudges of eye shadow that would feel damp because of her tears. Dez could remember kissing the top of her head, letting his lips find themselves surrounded by her burgundy-colored hair. "I love you, pumpkin," he would always say.

The images in Dez's mind were not matching the representation found in the mirror in front of him. The character of Dez a few months was so much more blissful; small, trivial things in life could not bother him. With Koral in his life, his mind remained unaffected by the harsh and lingering cruelty of the outside world.

Nowadays, that image had disappeared into a realm of dejection and despair. That version of Dez was now dead, buried in the depths of loss and heartbreak.

Dez felt the urge to smash his fist through the mirror, but a distant voice in the back of his mind helped resist the temptation to do so. *Don't do it, Dez.* His eyes were now staring through the mirror, his retinas fixated on the anger that surrounded the image of him in the mirror.

The voice was becoming louder. *You're letting her win, Dez.* Dez raised his fist, letting every finger crunch together while the veins protruded through his skin. *Everything happens for a reason, Dez.* His arm and bicep were bulging as he brought his fist further back. *You'll understand it soon enough, Dez.*

The boom of the dreary voice began to echo in his brain. *Let it go, Dez. Just let it go.* He didn't want to let it go. The indescribable pain that had encompassed his heart was almost visible in the mirror's reflection. *It's in your eyes, Dez. People can see the hurt in your eyes.* Dez shut his eyes and saw nothing but colluded red against a black background.

The voice would not let him carry out his violent action. *Don't do it, Dez. Be strong.* His fingers were starting to hurt within his clenched, poised fist. *Everything happens for a reason, Dez. You'll see soon enough.*

The voice faded into the distance beyond the barriers as of Dez's mind as he unclenched his fist and dropped down to the floor. Leaning on his knees, he pulled at his shirt and let the tears build up in his eyes. While each one fell to the ground of the carpeted bedroom floor, Dez watched out of the top of his vision into the mirror.

With hate-filled eyes, he stood up to his feet. With a quick and forward motion, he brought his right fist into the mirror. Shatters of glass broke in waves as they sliced the skin of Dez's hand. Droplets of blood squirted onto the standing pieces of mirror that were unaffected by the sharp blast of his punch.

With drool gathering on his bottom lip, Dez cried out in pain, bringing his punctured hand close to his chest, letting blood coat portions of his shirt. Pieces of demolished mirror lay on the floor around him. His tears continued to drip down his face, gelling with the drool that had already been forming near his chin.

Dez tore at the neck hole of his shirt and ripped it down the middle. Franticly throwing it off of him, it fell a few feet from his bed next to a scattered pile of CDs. He ran out of the room, holding his right hand as the blood dripped onto the tile floor of the hallway. He turned on the cold water in the bathroom sink and let the icy stream clean his wound.

The rays of sunlight glimmered amongst the pieces of mirror that were strewn across the bedroom floor. Some of the light was shining upon a half of a white star with a long red streak wavering down the middle.

*   *   *   *

"You know you shouldn't be eating that, kid. Shit like that is very unhealthy," she said.

Chester looked up while chewing bits of the cheeseburger that he bought on his lunch break. Betty was standing in front of the white counter he was leaning on, giving him that unwarranted sly smile she was known for.

"Believe me, babe, I've put much worse in this body of mine," he retorted with a grin.

Betty shushed him and continued to smile. "Oh, really? I think behind that "bad ass" exterior you're just a head case with too many things to prove to the world."

Chester laughed and wiped his mouth with a napkin. "Oh, is that right? And I think that if you were a few years younger you'd want to jump me in the back room."

Betty's face turned red and she gave him the middle finger. Grabbing her clipboard in front of her, she winced at Chester and walked away.

Chester brought his mouth down on the hunk of meat in front of him and clamped down his teeth, taking a huge chunk as he brought his head up. He glanced up at the clock while chewing and reached into his pocket. He felt around for his cell phone and pulled it out. There was a missed call from Johnny.

He tossed the phone to the side and refocused his energy on finishing the burger. It was almost two in the afternoon and the SRC was dead. During the summer months, some of the patients would be transferred to local support "homes" with normal families that, in Chester's opinion, had "way too much to give to the world."

The patients that could not be trusted remained indoors at the SRC. Patients like Jeremy, a red-headed 40-year-old with intermittent anger disorder, would have to watch the summer months from the barred windows in their rooms.

"Chester, can I have a bite?" asked a large figure from around the corner of the desk. Jeremy was wearing the standard white gown that all SC patients were required to wear, however, he liked to scrawl various objects onto the cloth with a black permanent marker.

Chester finished chewing what was in his mouth and swallowed. "Sorry Jeremy, didn't the orderly serve you lunch today?"

Jeremy's face frowned and he looked away. "I hate meatloaf. I hate it. I hate meatloaf." His hands were shaking in a rapid motion, and Chester became cautious. Jeremy's intermittent anger disorder caused him to become easily infuriated over the simplest of matters. One of the first times that Chester had encountered the patient, he was upset because Betty had thrown away a blue plastic fork that Jeremy was using to tear a hole in his bed sheet. He became enraged and flipped over the table in the day room across from his room.

Chester looked at the quarter of the cheeseburger that was left in its wrapping in front of him. "Sorry about the meatloaf, Jeremy," he said. "I overheard Betty talking about having brownies later for dessert. You like brownies, right?" Chester winked at the patient.

Jeremy started jumping up and down and clapping his hands. "I love brownies! I love brownies!" He ran down around the corner of the hall and up the stairs.

"Never a dull moment in this fucking place," Chester said to himself. His shift ended at six, and still he had no plans for the evening. He hadn't heard from Dez in nearly two days, and was hoping that his friend would be in a better mood on their next night out.

Chester's face was getting itchy; it was almost time for a fix. He hated working the first floor counter, as it never allowed him an opportunity to escape for 10 minutes if he needed to. Betty would not be back for at least another hour, and the other orderlies were on the other two floors.

It was times likes these that Chester thought about abandoning his drug use. The most ironic aspect of his substance abuse, according to Johnny, was that Chester seemed to have utter and total control over it.

He had grown up with a good family, always did very well in school, and ended up graduating at the top of his college class with a Bachelor's Degree in psychology. Going to school up in the boondocks of Maine presented Chester with a dilemma: he replaced his friends with drugs like crystal meth.

Chester always felt guilty for putting those toxins into his body, and swore to himself that once he was settled into a career he'd kick the habit once and for all. It only took him a few months to land a job within his field after graduating from college; the SRC was looking for young talent to grace their halls. Chester wasn't exactly desperate, but he jumped at the opportunity to welcome employment in the psychology field.

As annoying as some of the patients became, Chester still went home at the end of the day happy with his job. It also allowed him a chance to garner other drugs that could easily be traded for what he needed.

Perhaps that was the irony of Chester's life: he held a warming heart of gold that could easily fade into a black chunk of coal when he had to face his addictions. Deep down inside of his chest, all of the patience with the SRC and his willingness to assist the handicapped blew away in a wind of shadiness and malevolence when he snorted that long line of meth.

He could hear Jeremy shouting at someone beyond the hall around the right corner of the desk. Chester leaned and shook his head. He was looking forward to unwinding later on at night. In between games of solitaire on the computer in front of him, his mind focused on various bars that he and the others could go to.

Big Jim's Bar and Grill was always their fallback; whenever bigger plans fell through, the group met there to split a pizza and plenty of pitchers of beer. Plus it was hilarious to witness the countless Revmont barflies attempt to sing various Frank Sinatra songs on karaoke night.

The last time the group had gone to Big Jim's, Dez blacked out and they had to cut the night short. It probably wasn't a good idea to go back so soon.

Chester was yearning for something a little different for the evening. Betty was always talking about a place called Vincenzo's that was close to 20 miles outside Revmont. According to the nurse, it was a popular hangout for singles in their late 30s and 40s, although the getup was mostly made of divorced women looking for younger men to play "sugar momma" to.

I'll have to get directions from Betty, thought Chester. He smiled and turned his attention back to the solitaire game on the computer. If there's one thing that'll cheer up Dez, he thought, it's older women that want to fuck him.

Betty walked by in a hurry and Chester shouted at her. "Hey! Come over here for a second."

"What do you want? I need to administer three more sedations on the third floor and there may or may not be a bedpan or two to clean up." Her hair was brushed over a thin white bandanna and little drops of sweat were beginning to form near her brow.

"This Vincenzo's place you always tell me about…I need directions." Chester was grinning with a devious smile on his face.

"Oh, Chester, you and your buddies don't want to go there." Betty was staring at the two rows of white teeth that Chester was showing. "Believe me, you're better off going to one of those trendy bars in downtown Boston. People your age avoid Vincenzo's like it's the plague."

"That's the whole thrill, babe," Chester said. "It's something different. Plus we're trying to cheer my best friend Dez up. He's going through a nasty breakup and he could use some older, um, companionship and cuddling."

Betty scoffed and flipped back her hair into a bun. "Alright, fine, I'll give you directions. But, I say this now: don't bitch to me the next day and tell me that you were bored." Chester cheered and blew a kiss at Betty.

CHAPTER 7

▼

"I swear, Dane, if this is a joke, I'm going to be pissed." Professor Ulrich was gripping the phone with his right hand while his left hand formed a tight fist.

"Professor, I didn't sleep last night." Dane's voice sounded weak and raspy. "If that letter is real, we're all in for a world of hurt when Venus aligns with the sun and Earth."

"I just can't even fathom something like this. How the hell can something like that chaotic scene go unnoticed in history?" The professor was nearly shouting into the phone. Professor Levin, who held the office next door to his, was staring into his window. "I understand that it was well over 100 years ago, but don't you think that someone would uncover something like this?"

"Professor Ulrich, we may very well be the first people to read that letter since someone hid it away in that public records building." Dane tried to collect himself. It wasn't always easy dealing with the professor when he was frazzled.

"Bullshit." The professor felt the urge to hang up the phone and punch the wall. "Dane, I'm trying my best to be calm here. I must have sat on my living room couch horrified well into the night after reading that."

"Listen, I'll be at the university soon. Will be at your office in an hour?" asked Dane.

"Yeah, I'll be here." Professor Ulrich hung up the phone and sat down at his desk. Out of the corner of his eye, he saw a wave of blonde hair walk by his office. He crinkled his nose and leaned back in his chair.

Faith stuck her head in the doorway and smiled. "I knew it was the one after Levin's. You don't have a nametag on the office door." She was wearing tight jeans and a black tank-top. It looked as if she had gone tanning; her cleavage was a bronze color.

Professor Ulrich pushed his hands through his hair and let the front bangs droop into his eyes. "I'm not even going to ask what you're doing here, Faith."

"Bruce, you don't return my phone calls. You don't respond to my emails." Her big blue eyes twinkled in the bright office light. "Just because we're divorced doesn't mean we have to avoid each other completely."

Professor Ulrich felt rage encompass his body. "Oh, is that right? What the fuck are you on, Faith? Do you honestly believe that there's a need for us to be in contact with each other?"

Faith brought her lips closer together and looked away. "I always hated when you raised your voice, Bruce. It never sounded like you." Her arms crossed, she looked down at her black boots and took a deep breath. "I called you the other night because I was lonely. My friends act like they're ten years younger than they actually are. They don't know what it's like to be me."

"Don't walk into my office unannounced and nuisance me with your sanctimonious platitudes." Professor Ulrich stared directly into his ex-wife's eyes. "Faith, we're divorced. I'm moving on with my life, as you have been. Walk back out of that door and stay out. You've done enough damage."

Tears began to form in Faith's eyes as she brought her hands to her face. "I don't know, Bruce. There are times when I regret leaving you." It was hard to let the words flow out of her mouth with the tears finding their way down her cheeks.

"Don't even start. I have enough to worry about right now, Faith." Professor Ulrich turned his vision to the computer screen.

Faith turned around and walked out the door. The professor could hear her boots squeaking along the tile hallway outside of his office. He buried his face in his hands and let his head gently ease itself on his desk next to his keyboard.

It was bad enough that there might or might not be a looming threat when Venus aligns itself the next day, let alone an ex-wife trying to walk back into his life. Everything seemed to be too much for Professor Ulrich to handle; he was usually strong in most situations, but all of the pain he dealt with after the divorce somewhat damaged the walls around his robust nature.

He sighed and collected his thoughts. Faith. Insanity. Venus. Impending doom. The professor's mind floated into a dominion of rotten quandary. It was time to for him to take a breath and ease his mind. Professor Ulrich leaned back in his chair and decided to check his email.

*   *   *   *

The hot air of Revmont's busy streets flowed in and out of Nathan's car. The sounds of the Beastie Boys decorated the walls of his vehicle as he pulled up to a traffic light. He bobbed his head up and down with the beat of the song.

Nathan loved taking a half-hour break from work to take a ride in his car. He looked forward to driving in his Mustang every minute he was wasting away at the grocery store. He let the last track of the CD finish and slipped it back into its case when the stereo ejected it.

We're positive that there will be nothing out of the ordinary late tomorrow evening. Nathan must have flipped the radio dial to the AM frequency accidentally earlier in the morning while he was half-awake. *Astronomers have not had the opportunity to witness something like this since the late 1800s. It's going to be quite a sight. Venus only comes into this perfect alignment every 112 years.*

Nathan remembered seeing something on TV about Venus, but didn't pay attention to it. When he checked the local newspaper in the morning to read his daily horoscope, there was a one-page spread including an artist's interpretation of how it might look. Nathan glanced at it briefly, but wasn't too interested.

The fact of the matter remains that there are hundreds of thousands of people that have been looking forward to this event for months. Nathan winced at the broadcaster's annoying voice. "Who the fuck would get excited about something like that?" he asked himself aloud. He smiled and flipped off the radio dial.

Nathan passed by the apartment and wondered what his brother was up to. Nathan wished that Dez's character would be more appealing to the social world. Although he felt awful about his breakup with Koral, there was a part of him that wished his brother would just get over it already.

He looked at the clock on the dashboard. He only had ten minutes left on his break. Nathan turned left after the train station on the road he was on and made his way back in the direction of the grocery store.

Pulling up behind a station wagon, he fumbled with the radio dial until finding a station he liked. The grocery store was just around the corner.

Pulling into the parking lot and squeezing into a space near the entrance, he shut off the engine and leaned over to the passenger side seat to grab his bottle of water and his cell phone. Nathan groaned as the warming rays of the sun shined brightly into his eyes.

*   *   *   *

The sound of a car alarm outside the bedroom window aroused Dez out of his sound sleep. He shifted his weight over to his left side and stared at the mirror in the corner of the room; the few scarred pieces still attached gave off an uninviting glow.

Dez yawned and turned back over to his other side. The throbbing pain in his hand was gone, although he was sure that if he removed the bandage there might be enough blood to warrant an emergency room visit. Too bad I don't have health insurance, he thought to himself.

He wondered if Nathan was home yet. There were no sounds coming outside of his bedroom door, so he figured that he must be working.

Dez yawned again and sat up in his bed. The bed sheets were in disarray; his heavy quilt was tossed about the opposite side of the bed and the bed lining had come off the bottom of the bed, revealing the rough surface of the mattress underneath.

He reached into his shorts and adjusted his underwear. Throwing his feet over the side of bed, he slowly touched the ground and attempted to stand up. Dez scratched his right shoulder and walked over the pieces of broken mirror lying on the bedroom floor.

Dez picked up the bigger shards of glass and flung them into the wastebasket near the doorway. With eyes fixated on the mess that was the area of disaster, he shook his head and walked out of the bedroom.

The pile of broken mirror pieces combined with the sight that used to be his favorite t-shirt send chills up and down Dez's spine. He had never once imagined life without Koral during the entire length of their blissful relationship; it seemed that as if the entire ride was just a trip on a cloud high above the real world, a place where happiness reigned without the looming threat of misery and failure.

Dez walked into the kitchen and peered outside. With a sigh, his mind wandered back into thoughts of just a few months ago.

With the spring season on the horizon, Dez was feeling somewhat jovial. He had been doing some freelance work for a few local newspapers and was able to live off the little money that he was getting paid per article. He had saved up enough cash to still be able to pay the rent and make a couple trips out to Chicago to see Koral.

Dez reflected upon those moments while he was looking out into the hot summer sun. Bright light garnished the street in front of his apartment. People going about their daily business were walking by. He sighed and reminisced.

The last time Dez had seen Koral was the weekend of Easter. Work was picking up quickly after spring had started, and he found himself carousing around to three different Revmont newspapers with various story ideas and news-related happenings.

He remembered how proud Koral was of him; her boyfriend was starting to make a little progress in his field. She, on the other hand, was working the same unpleasant job she had always been a part of since their relationship started. It always bothered Dez that Koral had no drive to succeed in life; her idea of conformability with life consisted of the very things she had: her dog, her family and friends, and of course, Dez.

Dez brushed his hair back with his hand and thought about that last weekend with her. After spending the morning in Revmont City Hall trying to brush up on zoning laws for a story, he went back to his apartment to pack for the trip.

The train ride to the airport was always one of anticipation for Dez; the tired looks on the passengers' faces that day would not alter his mood in any shape or form. He was going to see his love, and that was all that had encompassed his mind.

Sitting in the terminal, waiting for his plane to board, Dez had called Koral and left her a voicemail telling her that he was about to board the plane, and that he couldn't wait to see her. With an "I love you, babe," he shut off his cell phone and put his headphones on.

The echoic verses of Bono drove the custom U2 mix into Dez's brainwaves.

The plane ride on that crisp April evening was one that Dez would never forget; in his mind, it was just another heartwarming weekend with the love of his life. Little did he know at the time that it would also be the last he would spend with her.

Spending Easter weekend with Koral was something Dez had looked forward to since the moment she had left Boston after Valentine's Day weekend. Stepping off the plane in Chicago at O'Hare, he calmly fixed his spikey black hair in a bathroom mirror and made his way to the baggage claim area to greet his girlfriend.

There was something different in her eyes that time, Dez could remember. Koral did not seem herself at all; the first embracing kiss on that April night in her car didn't have the same fire as it normally did.

Dez could almost taste the strawberry lip gloss in his mouth right now. The memories inside of his head were so vivid that he could often escape to that dreary world without warning or evading his current situation. This was a problem; he was never going to be fine again until he could fully shake her ghostly presence in his life.

Dez traveled further into the back of his mind. He thought about the last times he would ever penetrate Koral; the last times they made love seemed like the closest he had ever been to another human being. The glisten of sweat on his biceps, the way her red hair would fall out of its ponytail formation when she went down on him, the nail marks left on Dez's back while she achieved multiple orgasms, it all circled around his head now like a sick and twisted version of a "keep away" game.

Dez sat down at the kitchen table and let his bangs fall forward into his face. The thought of sex with Koral was now making him sick. All he could picture every time he thought about it was another asshole digging into the woman he once thought he'd spend the rest of his life with. Feelings of rage filled Dez's head; all he wanted to do was feel the quaint satisfaction from punching someone in the face.

The quiet sounds of the outside world were trying to mellow the mood inside of the belligerent nature of the apartment. Dez could feel his mind slipping back into a deep melancholy. He closed and eyes and got up from the kitchen table.

Walking over to the living room, he plopped himself down on the couch and let the leather stick to his thighs. With a small ripping sound, he aligned his position to lay down with his left foot hanging near the top of the couch.

Dez thought about that fateful morning when Koral had broken up with him. Waking up after a long evening with Chester and Johnny, he arose to hear his cell phone ringing. Dez was confused and rubbed the sleep out of his eyes before opening it.

Word by word, he heard her with shock and the beginnings of small tears began to form in his gentle heart. As each line was read, Dez had felt his chest slowly burn and hollow out; leaving nothing but his tears to fill the hole.

"What the fuck Koral!" was the only scream Dez could let out of his meager voice box after the conversation with his now ex-girlfriend. Every single notion of the future, every solitary moment of fidelity and happiness, every moment the two had spent together floated in his Dez's mind as he sat speechless in the corner of his bed, not knowing what to do.

By the time Koral had called him that afternoon, Dez had done his share of crying; he just wanted the cold truth, no matter how much it hurt on the way in.

"I'm not in love with you Dez," she had said. The sun was shining brightly, Dez could remember with a vibrant eye. Koral had fallen out of love with him, and there was nothing he could do to salvage the relationship. He wasn't a bad boyfriend in any way; he had always cared for her with 100 percent of heart.

"I don't feel the same way about you that I did last summer," Koral said to him. A million different possibilities were spinning in his head at the time. Had their relationship gotten so comfortable that the romance and love found its way out? It killed Dez to hear that she wasn't in love with him anymore. The thousands of times he expressed his love for Koral might as well have been for nothing; a year with her was a wasted one, and now he had to deal with the pain and agony of being without her on his own.

Dez snapped back into the realm of reality. He brought his hands over his face, brushing back his bangs and letting his chest breathe in and out. He needed to get away from it all, he thought to himself. Where he would go was the only question in his mind.

Peering outside the living room window, Dez caught a glimpse of an elderly couple sitting on the bench near the bus stop across the street from the apartment. He could clearly see that they were still in love. The old man had his left arm draped around his wife, who was smiling as she clutched her silver cane closer to her thigh.

The woman's gray hair was pulled back into a ponytail. Her husband leaned over to give her a kiss and grinned from ear to ear after doing so.

For a moment, Dez wanted to put a bullet through each of their skulls.

CHAPTER 8

▼

Dane sped faster towards the highway. He was already 15 minutes late for his meeting with the professor, and was hoping that the rush hour traffic wouldn't make matters worse.

On the highway, he switched lanes quickly to get to the far left. Once there, he pressed against the gas pedal with full force until the odometer reached the 80 miles per hour mark. With the windows of his pickup truck down, the harsh winds quickly weaved in and out of the vehicle, tossing Dane's brown hair in different directions.

Speeding in between other cars on the highway, Dane tried his best to stay focused on the road. He almost never drove as fast as he was now; getting a speeding ticket from the Massachusetts State Police always scared the shit out of him, especially since he was already behind on insurance payments for his car.

"Come on, move!" Dane shouted to the car in front of him. The small compact car in front of him was going no more than 40 miles an hour. Straining his eyes, Dane could make out an elderly woman behind the wheel. "Great! I'm stuck behind this goddamn geezer and I'm already late. The professor is going to strangle me."

Pressing the gas pedal harder than he was before, Dane swerved to the right and passed the old woman that was in front of him. Scratching his right thigh, he signaled to the right to get in the far right lane.

The exit to the university was just up ahead.

*   *   *   *

Professor Ulrich sat in the chair behind his desk and stared at the computer screen. The box score for last night's Red Sox game was in the center, surrounded by pictures and other statistics from the team's win over the Orioles the night before.

With a groan, he sat back and put his feet up on the desk. He looked in the small mirror that sat on his desk and took a deep breath. My eyes are bloodshot, he thought to himself. Pulling the bottom of his eyelid down and bringing his face closer to the mirror, the professor realized his eyes were indeed bloodshot.

All he could think about was Faith and whether or not the letter was real. His thoughts jumped back and forth from his ex-wife to the child who wrote the letter. The biggest thing she's worried about is whether or not I hate her, and all I'm worried about is what the hell is going to happen tomorrow night, the professor thought.

He stared back into the mirror. "No one's going to believe you, Bruce," he said to himself while shaking his head. It was true, and not only did Bruce have a thousand questions for that letter, he still had the burden of how to approach it.

The professor glanced at his watch and realized that Dane was over 20 minutes late. He eased himself out of the chair like an old man and walked over to the small fridge. He pulled out a beer and twisted off the cap. "And they tell college students not to drink in their dorms," he said aloud with a laugh.

He heard a shuffle and a large thud outside his office door and jogged over to investigate. Swinging open the door to his office, he saw Dane kneeled down on the floor, clutching various papers and trying to adjust his thick, black-framed glasses.

Professor Ulrich chuckled and looked over at his graduate assistant. "That's exactly what I needed to cheer me up, Dane. Thanks a lot."

Dane rolled his eyes and looked up the professor. "Ha ha, very funny professor. I was running over here because I was late and took a spill." He was franticly fumbling around for all of the papers that fell out of his backpack. His eyes caught the bottle of beer in the professor's right hand. "You're not supposed to be drinking on campus," he said with a sly smile.

The professor grinned and took a swig of beer. It felt cold on the inside of his throat. "Please, *you* try dealing with an ex-wife, too many students, and God knows what else," he said. He took another gulp and felt the coolness settle inside of his stomach.

Dane had finally gathered all of his belongings that had fallen. "Professor, I really think we need to analyze that letter." He fixed the collar of his tight green mohair sweater. "The nerdy scientist in both of us is getting the best of our conscious thinking if this is actually some sort of joke."

Professor Ulrich tilted his head to the side and looked directly into Dane's eyes. "Dane, buddy, most of the time, that nerdy scientist in both us is usually right." His fingers were gripping the neck of the beer bottle. "I've been through so much shit this past year that I would believe almost anything nowadays."

His mind drifted away for a moment. The professor had a quick flash of vision of Faith in her wedding dress. He took a long swig of the beer and finished it off, leaning down and balancing it against the corridor wall to his left.

Dane felt the phlegm in his mouth slither down back into his throat. "Professor, I know you've been going through a lot with your ex-wife and all, but I really think that we need to take a closer look at this letter."

"Sounds good, come into my office and pull up a chair," Professor Ulrich said while jiggling the change in his front pockets.

Dane walked into the office and threw his bag down onto the guest chair opposite of where he was going to sit. He unzipped the large section of the bag and pulled out a yellow notepad. He flipped through the first few pages and scratched his head.

"Well? What've you got for me?" Professor Ulrich removed his suit jacket and revealed his pale arms that were normally hidden under the black blazer that he always wore around the university. His black Guns N' Roses "Use Your Illusion Tour 1992" shirt was exceptionally faded in most areas.

Dane pulled a pen out of his bag and scribbled something on the notepad. "One thing I was thinking of was this: under the assumption that this document is the real deal, there's always the possibility of this Hilda character was mentally unstable and just writing what she wrote for pleasure, not for the sake of actuality." He shrugged his shoulders and shook his head. "Well?"

Professor Ulrich licked his lips and looked over at the computer screen. He turned his attention back over to Dane and nodded his head. "We're missing something obvious here, kiddo. The first thing we should have done is had these two pieces of paper tested to see how old they *actually* are."

Dane smacked the side of his own head and jumped up out of chair. "Shit! I can't believe we didn't even think of that!"

Professor Ulrich smiled at Dane. "Sometimes even the simplest things are lost to notions that don't really matter in our lives, Dane." He pointed to a picture of Faith and himself from one of their camping trips a couple years back. "You're young and intelligent. Do me a favor and keep your eye on the science ball; don't let a woman ruin that for you."

Dane let himself smile and looked away. He sometimes felt as though the professor was a mentor to him. They were closer than the average college professor and student. They would often catch a few beers at the pub around the corner from NBU and spend hours debating over certain scientific theories.

"Thanks for the tip professor, I know those females can sometimes be trouble for us scientists," Dane said as he readjusted his glasses. Although was a bit of fear over the letter, he felt safe working on the problem with the professor, as if he wouldn't let Dane down no matter what the situation.

The professor pulled out the long manila enveloped that contained the letter and eased it down onto the desk. Both he and Dane stared at it for a minute. "Well, I'll call Clancy down at the lab to see how long it would take to correctly date this thing. We've got a pretty good lab here. It shouldn't be too long."

Dane nodded in agreement. "Sounds good. Is there anything we should do in the meantime, Professor?" His big brown eyes were fixated on the professor.

Professor Ulrich sighed and stretched his arms. "Just hang out, focus on your work for the rest of the day. The alignment won't be happening until late tomorrow night."

"Okay, Professor. I'll give you a call later to check in," Dane said. He packed up his notes and zipped the black bag closed. He stood up and placed the bag over both shoulders and his back.

"I'll call Clancy now. As soon as I hear something, I'll let you know," said the professor. Dane said bye and walked out of the office, closing the door on his way out.

Professor Ulrich reached into his desk drawer and searched for his date planner. He couldn't remember Clancy's number. Sitting underneath two nearly empty packs of cigarettes and few magazines, the professor found his planner.

Fumbling through the pages, he rummaged around to the back, where all of his NBU numbers were kept. "Clancy Wakefield, where are you?" the professor asked himself aloud. "There you are."

Sitting on one of the final pages in the planner was two of Clancy's phone numbers, one for his cell phone and the other for the lab at NBU. The professor dialed the lab number and waited as the other line rang. The office was starting to get cold, and he put his suit jacket back on.

"Clancy Wakefield," the deep, raspy voice on the other line said.

"Clancy, my friend, it's Bruce," said the professor.

"Bruce, how are you? What can I do for you buddy?" Clancy's voice always reminded the professor of a bookie.

"I'm doing fine. Listen, I need a favor."

"Sure, Bruce, I still owe you for helping me out with neuroscience project last year," said Clancy. "What do you need?"

"I have a letter that was supposedly written over a hundred years ago. What I need is to find out if it's actually that *old*." Professor Ulrich's voice became serious.

Clancy coughed and there was silence for abut thirty seconds. "Wow, a one-hundred-year-old letter. Jesus, Bruce. Where the hell did you get *that*?" There was a sense of disbelief in his voice.

"It's a long story. How long will it take for you to date this thing?" Professor Ulrich placed all of his trust in Clancy's answer.

Clancy coughed again. "That depends. How many pieces of paper in total?"

"It's only two," replied the professor. "They're both in mint condition. My graduate assistant found them buried away in a public records library."

"I'll be here for another couple of hours. Run it down here and hopefully I'll have something for by tomorrow afternoon."

Professor Ulrich let out a massive sigh. "Thank you so much, Clancy."

Clancy said goodbye and hung up the phone. The professor looked at the envelope and ran his index finger up and down the side. "Okay, Hilda. Let's find out how old you *really* are."

*   *   *   *

Johnny gripped the bottle of Vanilla Coke and stared at the ceiling. He hated picking up Chester from work. There was something about the SRC that had completely grossed him out. The smell of hospitals and moth balls sent too many chills through his skin.

The sights of mentally challenged individuals walking by him wearing blue gowns made him wince with disgust. "Chester, where are you, buddy?" Johnny whispered to himself as he looked at the clock down the hall.

A man who had slobbered what looked like some sort of tomato sauce on the front of his gown jogged past Johnny. A chubby nurse with long black hair writing on a clipboard followed the man and screamed after him. For a second, he wondered how his friend dealt with this place on a daily basis.

Out of the corner of his eye, Johnny saw Chester walking up and putting on his green khaki jacket. Johnny took a sip of his drink and stood up.

"Well, it's about fucking time, dude!" Johnny's arms were outstretched and he had a frown on his face.

"Sorry, man. I have to go take care of something, I'll be right back." Chester winked at his friend and trotted towards the staircase around the corner.

Johnny rolled his eyes and sat back down. After drinking the rest of his beverage, he pictured Chester huddled over a small piece of tinfoil, clearing out his nostrils to snort what was inside.

He could recall the first time Chester had told him that he had started doing drugs. It seemed like such an intense fallacy; Chester had grown up within a good family, had always done really well in school, and was doing well in college.

"Johnny, bro, I've been snorting crystal meth for a few months now." The words came during one of Chester's routine phone calls back home to Boston during the long semesters of his college run. Every week, he'd call Dez and then him, keeping them both up to date with what was happening at school. Johnny had never expected one of his best friends to be hooked on cocaine, let alone the meth Chester was inhaling at the very moment.

About ten minutes later, Chester re-emerged from the hallway with a grin on his face. His eyes were a tad bit glazed over and he was sweating, Johnny could notice. "I've got a perfect idea for tomorrow night," he said after sitting down next to his friend.

"Oh, really? And what's that?" Johnny's lips were closed tightly together and his eyebrows were almost inverted. Chester's ideas were always somewhat out of the ordinary. He could remember one of his suggestions last summer. Chester had found a 24-hour bowling alley owned by the Chinese mafia that was a three-hour drive from Revmont.

"There's this place called Vincenzo's that's about an hour's drive away from here." Chester had an energized look on his face. "Betty, a nurse that works with me, always goes there."

"Wait a second, isn't she in her 40s?" Johnny questioned.

Chester giggled and nodded his head. "The youngest women that go to this place are in their mid-30s." He now had engaged in a full smile.

"That's not my jive, dude." Johnny closed his eyes and put his head down. "Why would we want to go to a bar that only middle-aged women go to?"

"There you go, right there," Chester said with a hearty laugh. "Not only will it cheer Dez up a bit, I can guarantee you we'll have a blast. And just maybe, maybe, one of us will end up with a sugar momma for a night."

Johnny shoved Chester and shook his head. "You're nuts, bro. You drive, though."

Chester smiled and scratched his chin. "It's a deal. Dez is going to love this place."

CHAPTER 9

▼

Dez let the last three strings of the guitar reverberate in his left hand. He couldn't remember the last time he had picked it up. It felt good to hammer out a few riffs in his room and let his mind slip away for a little while.

The black polish on Dez's guitar shined brightly against the beams of sun that were traveling into his room. The down-tuned tones of the guitar filled the empty room. Dez could remember at one point in his life where all he really wanted to do with his life was write songs and play guitar in a rock band.

Nathan was at work, he had an early morning shift that would keep him out of the apartment until the late afternoon. Dez's brother was an avid drummer; he had always felt that the two shared a musical connection that he would never part with. After graduating college, Dez had pretty much given up the rock star dream and let his focus drift into becoming a journalist.

Ever since the breakup with Koral, he had let his dreams fall into a ravine of no return; hope for success seemed like an out-of-reach delusion. Dez's subconscious would not allow itself to pry off of the pain that had encompassed his heart for these past couple months.

Dez put down the guitar and sighed. He walked out of his room and into the kitchen, feeling tired even though he had done nothing to exert his energy. Chester had left him a voicemail earlier in the morning that said he'd be dropping by with Johnny sometime in the afternoon.

Friday afternoons were always lax in nature for Dez; he would normally spend them running errands or working out. There was some excitement for the weekend on these types of Fridays; however, Dez had not felt that joy in quite some time.

He missed drunken Friday nights in downtown Boston, and coming home and talking to Koral while slurring his words. She thought it was adorable, Dez thought to himself. Nowadays, drunken nights meant depressed and hung-over mornings. There was no one to find his inebriated actions cute and charming, he was on his own, which was hard to accept.

Dez felt extremely insecure when entering the highly social world outside of his apartment. In his mind, Koral was the climax of his lifelong search for romance; he would never again find someone so beautiful and endearing.

Chester would often sit him down and attempt to have a heart-to-heart conversation whenever they were together and alone. He had always told Dez that although the twinge in his heart felt so real and so vivid, there'd be other women to "fuck him and love him," as he would say.

"Chill out for a bunch of months and do your own thing," Chester would say. "You're young and good-looking. Not to mention that you've got incredible friends that would die for you." Dez smiled as he thought of his best friend's words of advice.

He thought into the future and wondered who else would be able to love someone like himself. Koral was the perfect woman; she had a bright smile that could warm his heart. The level of their attraction was astounding, Dez recalled the amazing sex he and Koral had experienced together.

Dez took a deep breath and pondered how long it was going to take to get over Koral. Time was his enemy; he wanted to destroy it with every ounce of mental strength he had. He remembered how hurt Johnny was when his friend had dealt with similar painful emotions after a severe breakup. Dez had honestly believed that he would never undergo that level of heartache with Koral; the most she would ever hurt him was by getting back on a plane after a visit.

Even dealing with that sort of pain was somewhat bearable for Dez, as there was always that next trip to look forward to. Living without her forever was unfathomable in his mind; it was something that he would never imagine dealing with.

Dez heard his cell phone ring in the other room. He jogged over to the bedroom and picked it up after several rings, answering it with a loud "Hello?"

"Hey dude, it's Chester," the voice on the other end replied.

"Hey bro, what's up?" Dez asked.

Chester took a sip out of his bottle of water. "Johnny just picked me up from work and we're going to head over to your place soon. I just need to make a stop somewhere first."

"Sounds good. I'll see you guys soon." Dez hung up the phone and threw it on the bed amongst a scattered pile of t-shirts and his thick quilt.

He walked back into the kitchen and opened the refrigerator. Searching through the shelves, he found nothing that would satisfy his hunger. Slamming the door shut, he grunted and decided to go outside and check his mail.

After opening the front door, he reached over to the mailbox and flipped open its metal lid. Dez peered in and found nothing but a menu from the Chinese restaurant down the street from his apartment. He grabbed it and walked back into the house.

Dez tossed the menu on the kitchen table and headed into the living room. After sitting down on the couch, he reached for the remote and turned the television on. He watched a few minutes of the replay of last night's Red Sox game and quickly became bored. He figured that he should probably take a shower before his friends arrived.

Dez removed his clothes upon entering the bathroom and turned on the shower. He let the waves of water from the massager ease the tension in his shoulders as he scrubbed his body with a facecloth.

After washing the soap off of his body, he heard the front door slam. "Dez! I'm home" Nathan screamed from the kitchen.

Nathan had just finished a long day of work at the grocery store. If there was one sight he was sick of, it was the sight of old women complaining about the quality of the fruit in the store. Nathan swore that there were at least eight or nine of this type of elderly women that had bothered him today.

He stretched his arms and yawned. Dez walked out of the bathroom wearing a white towel around his waist, his black hair dripping wet and drops of water hitting the ground. "Hey, fun day at work?" he asked his brother while fixing the knot on the towel.

"Oh, definitely," Nathan replied. "The next old woman I see with a cantaloupe in her hand I'm going to punch in the goddamn face." He yawned again and picked up the menu that Dez had left on the table.

Dez chuckled and grabbed a towel from the closet inside of his bedroom. He dried off his hair, leaving a shaggy mess on top of his head. "Come on dude, it can't be that bad. At least you're employed somewhere," he said while looking around his room for a pair of jeans. "I'm just about ready to start cleaning up vomit at a custodian with my journalism degree in my back pocket."

Nathan smiled and continued to flip the pages of the Chinese restaurant menu. "Well, at least you have a *degree*," he replied to his older brother. "I wonder if this place has good General Gau's chicken."

"I sincerely doubt it." Dez walked into the kitchen wearing torn stressed jeans and a plain white undershirt. "Chester and Johnny are coming by soon, are you hanging around here for a while?"

Nathan had finished thumbing through the menu. "Yeah, I'll be around for a while. I might be going to see a movie with Lauren later, but that's about all." He got up and walked into the living room, where the replay of the Red Sox game had entered the seventh inning. "These fucking Sox better get on the ball before the Yankees pull away in their division."

"I know. Wakefield pitched a good game last night but they absolutely sucked after Francona took him out," Dez called out from his bedroom, where he was looking through his drawers for a pair of black socks.

As Nathan got up to get something to drink from the kitchen, he heard a knock at the door. Opening the wooden door, he saw Chester plant his bare chest flush against the glass door, pulling his blue t-shirt up near his head. Nathan laughed and let the pair in.

Chester and Johnny walked into the apartment and shut the door behind them. "Where's big brother?" he asked Nathan, who was pouring a glass of iced tea in the kitchen.

"He's in his room I think." Nathan took a long sip of out the yellow plastic cup.

Dez walked out of his room and gave Johnny a pat on the back. "Hey guys, what's it like outside?"

Johnny turned around and gave his friend a high five. "It's not too bad out, I hear it might rain later though." He adjusted the collar of his tight white dress shirt.

Chester walked over and gave Dez a playful punch to the arm. "We've got something awesome planned for tomorrow night, dude. Let's just say we're all going to have one hell of a blast." His grin seemed a little too suspicious for Dez.

"Every time you smile like that, I get the feeling that I'm in for something strange." Dez rolled his eyes and then stared directly at Chester, who had left the room to rummage through the cabinets.

"You guys have no food in here," he said while sifting through a few boxes of cereal and an old jar of peanut butter. "Dez, just don't worry about it. Everything is in my hands."

"That exactly what worries me, dude." Dez walked into the kitchen. "There's got to be something in there, just keep looking."

Nathan directed Chester to a week-old bag of potato chips that was on the very top shelf inside of the cabinets. "Ah, here we go," Chester said while sticking his hand into the bag, crinkling the edges as he pulled out a handful of chips.

"So, anyways," Chester said while crunching on the bits of chips in his mouth, "there's this place called Vincenzo's."

*   *   *   *

Professor Ulrich sat at a table in the NBU coffee shop and stared past a group of students sitting directly across from him. The visions of a Bostonian dusk engulfed his vision. He took a sip of his coffee and pushed away the newspaper in front of him, which had a small story on the front page concerning tomorrow night's Venus alignment.

The professor laughed to himself after reading the first paragraph of the article. Taking another sip of coffee, he turned and faced the sight of the red clouds that hung over the sky. He looked at his watch and wondered how Clancy was making out with the dating for the letter.

After finishing the remnants of the coffee, the professor got up and threw the newspaper in the trash. A student ordering coffee at the counter recognized him and grabbed the sleeve of his suit jacket.

Gloria was in his astronomy class last semester. Standing at a little over five feet, the professor towered over her. "Hey Professor, I haven't seen you in a while! How are things going?" Her white smile was gleaming in the coffee shop light.

The professor looked down at her cleavage and quickly looked up at her eyes. "Hello Gloria. Things are going well, I was just stopping over here for a cup of coffee. I have some papers to grade for the first summer session."

"That's good. Are you excited about the Venus alignment tomorrow night? A few of my roommates and I are going to be watching the entire thing from the roof of the dorms." She continued to smile as the cashier handed her change.

Professor Ulrich let out a fake grin and looked away. "I'm definitely excited, Gloria. Although I don't have quite as exciting plans are you for the event." He glimpsed at her cleavage again. "I'm sorry, I have to run. Throw me an email sometime."

"Ok, see you soon, Professor," Gloria replied with yet another smile.

Professor Ulrich exited out the front door of the coffee shop and began walking to his car. He searched his front pocket for his keys and pulled them out. The reddish orange clouds overhead provided a perfect backdrop for the professor's mood.

He wished that things were the way there were a couple of years ago. Everything in life was nearly perfect for the professor; being with Faith stirred a constant happy notion in his heart, not to mention how he loved being a professor at NBU.

Professor Ulrich leaned on the hood of his car and wondered if he should have acted differently when Faith had approached him earlier in the day. She looked incredible, he thought to himself as he watched the colored clouds overhead slowly pass him by. It reminded him of the time when the two had spent the professor's winter break in California.

He flashed back to thoughts of holding Faith close to him as she fell asleep under the clear skies of the west coast. He sighed and pulled out his cell phone. Scrolling down to her number in his phone book, he paused before pressing the "send" button on the phone.

Professor Ulrich had a vision of Faith sitting in her car crying after he had told her off and told her to leave his office. He suddenly recalled the past year of living alone and decided that the pain she had put him through warranted his previous actions.

He slid off the hood of his car and opened the driver's side door, then threw the cell phone on the passenger's side seat next his bag.

The professor looked up to the sky. He saw nothing but orange as he started the engine to the car.

*   *   *   *

Chester chugged the beer in his right hand as he flipped through the television stations with the remote in his other. "There should be a Red Sox game every night, now there's nothing on at all."

Nathan gave him a funny look and put his feet up on the coffee table. "One-hundred and sixty-two games in six months, I think they deserve a break every now and again." He had changed into gray sweatpants but left his green work shirt on.

Chester frowned and continued to flip through the channels. He left the local newscast on as he got up to head into the kitchen.

What astronomers are calling perhaps the best outer space transit in history will take place late tomorrow evening as Venus will eclipse in an alignment with the earth and the sun. The celestial rarity has stargazers across the world in joyful anticipation.

Dez popped his head from out of the kitchen to take a better listen to the newscast. His attention sparked after recalling seeing a bunch of articles on Venus within recent weeks. He walked into the living room and focused his attention on the anchorwoman.

Venus makes two passes across the sun, eight years apart, every 122 years. The next one will happen in 2012. The sight will be somewhat visible without a semi-powerful telescope. We talked to Norwegian astronomer Jergaen Ortagaard, who has been preparing for this event since the beginning of the year.

Dez's eyes fixated on the television broadcast as he brought a bottle of beer to his mouth to take a gulp.

"No human alive today has ever seen such a transit, as the last such one happened well over a hundred years ago," said Ortagaard. "Not only is this event rare, it is also an opportunity to really appreciate such a cosmic infrequency within our own solar system." The astronomer believes that the public should share such a fascination and take a strong interest in taking the time to view it when it happens.

For all us here in Boston, the Harvard Smithsonian Center for Astrophysics in Cambridge will be allowing patrons to view the Venus transit through telescopes on the building's rooftop.

"I didn't know you were into scientific shit." Dez turned to his left and saw Johnny standing there, gripping a bottle of Jack Daniel's in hand.

"And I didn't know you were into Jack Daniel's, asshole," Dez replied with a laugh. "This Venus thing seems pretty cool. We'll probably be able to see it as we stumble around drunk after this Vincenzo's place closes tomorrow night." He took another sip of beer and threw his arm around the left armrest of the couch.

Scientists all over the world are encouraging everyone interested to view the rare phenomenon when it occurs tomorrow night. We will have coverage following the event on our morning broadcast.

Dez finished off the bottle of beer and placed it on the glass coffee table in front of him. Chester wandered into the living room and sat down next to him. He picked up the remote and changed the channel, finding a stand-up comedy show on one of the cable stations.

"How are you feeling, dude?" Chester asked Dez.

Dez looked at his friend and shrugged his shoulders. "It's a weird feeling, Chester. It almost feels as if I'm in limbo; I'm stuck between my past and trying to move on with my life." He brushed back his bangs with his hands and placed his head back on the cushion of the couch.

"I know how you feel, bro." Chester gave a small smile and leaned forward. "All joking aside, it really hurts all of us to see you like this. Johnny, Nathan and I are not trying to rush your progress along when we say we want to cheer you up." He had a stern yet compassionate look on his face.

Dez managed to gather a grin for his best friend. "I understand that, bro. Believe me, I appreciate everything you guys have done for me. I would have killed myself a long time ago if I didn't have the support I've had in you guys." All of the bottled-up emotion inside of chest began to creep up into voice.

Chester could feel the tension in Dez's voice. "Hang in there, Dez. Everything will work itself out in the end." His smile revealed the amount of care in his voice. "You never know what's going to happen. Everything happens for a reason, bro. Just give it some time."

Dez sighed and gave Chester a pat on his knee. He got up off of the couch and made his way into the kitchen to get another beer. Nathan and Johnny were playing a game of Texas Hold'em.

"Shit, that queen is going to completely fuck me up," Nathan said after tossing in a few poker chips into the small pile in the center of the table. Johnny laughed and poured the rest of his Vanilla Coke into a plastic cup, mixing it with the Jack Daniel's.

Dez leaned over Nathan's shoulder to see that he was holding a five of clubs and a jack of hearts. "No peeking, bitch," Johnny said after taking a sip of his new concoction. Dez opened the fridge and grabbed a bottle of beer.

From the kitchen, he could hear Chester changing the stations on the television, not finding a single channel to hold his attention. Dez walked into the living room and grabbed the remote out of hand.

*   *   *   *

Professor Ulrich sat at the kitchen table in his apartment with an uneaten plate of leftover chicken and rice in front of him. He didn't have much of an appetite with all of the thoughts swirling around in his head. Not only that, his once-a-week cooking and leftovers were nothing to be desired.

Ever since his divorce with Faith, he relied mostly on healthy frozen dinners and take out for dinner every evening.

He pushed the plate of food away and got up out of his seat at the table. Walking over to the refrigerator, he reached into it to pull out the bottle of wine that he had opened a few weeks ago to celebrate the end of the semester.

The professor opened up the cabinet above the kitchen sink and looked for a wine glass. Finding one that suited his taste, he grabbed it and poured himself a full glass of the merlot. He walked into the living room and sat on the long couch against the wall. Kicking off his Doc Martens, he spread his legs out over the cushion and leaned against the armrest.

Taking a long sip out of the glass, the professor closed his eyes and thought about tomorrow night. Quickly, his thoughts vanished into a realm of Faith and the past year. He attempted to remove the thoughts from his mind, but failed to do so.

His mind fixated on the way Faith had looked when she had stopped by his office. She was just as gorgeous as the day they had split up. The glowing image of her body stayed within the context of the professor's mind. He missed sex with Faith; he missed sex as a whole for that matter. It had been almost a year since he last had experienced it, as the last person he had slept was Faith.

Professor Ulrich snapped his mind out of fornicating his ex-wife and took another sip of wine. He brought his mental attention back to Venus and the letter. He wondered what kind of news Clancy would have for him in the morning.

The professor stood up and walked over to his music collection on the wall of the living room. Some music will help me relax, he thought.

Thumbing through the CDs in the tower, he passed by numerous bands. He pulled out Mötley Crüe's *Greatest Hits* album but realized he wasn't in the mood for anything too loud or heavy.

He passed on Bon Jovi and Guns N' Roses, as well as Nine Inch Nails. Professor Ulrich finally settled on U2's *Acthung Baby* disc and removed it from the CD tower. He placed the album into the deluxe stereo system in the living room and put the volume up a little bit.

"I'm ready for the laughing gas," crooned Bono as the professor drank his wine on the couch. The moonlight shined brightly on the streets outside. He looked outside and let his mind drift away.

CHAPTER 10

▼

The sound of jackhammers awoke the professor out of his sound sleep. He jumped up off the couch and realized that he was still wearing his clothes from the previous day. He must have fallen asleep in them, he thought.

The empty wine glass on the coffee table reflected the incoming sunlight into the professor's eyes. He squinted and picked it up. The red light on his stereo system caught his eye; he drifted into slumber last night as U2's music played on.

Professor Ulrich rubbed the sleep out of his eyes and walked into the kitchen. The digital clock on top of the stove read 9:16. He wasn't used to sleeping this late, he would normally would have already been at the gym for an hour on a normal Saturday morning.

Walking past his bedroom on the way to the bathroom, he heard his cell phone vibrating in his coat pocket. He hurriedly picked up but ended up missing the call. Clancy had called and left a voicemail for the professor.

Dialing his voicemail, he walked into the bathroom and turned on the water in the shower. "Bruce, it's Clancy, I've got some news on your mystery letter. I'll be at the lab all day, stop by when you can."

Professor Ulrich felt a small rush of apprehension grip his body as he hung up the phone and placed it on the bathroom sink counter. He removed his clothes and stepped into the shower.

The hot water woke him up as he lathered his body with cucumber melon gel. Frantic thoughts rushed through his mind; thoughts of Faith, thoughts of undead creatures tearing apart Hilda and her father, and thoughts of watching Venus passing by the sun.

After stepping out of the shower, the professor reached for a towel and dried himself off. He picked up the cell phone on the sink counter and dialed Dane's number. The call went straight to his assistant's voicemail.

"Hey Dane, it's Professor Ulrich. It's almost 9:30 in the morning, I'll be on my way to see Clancy from the lab soon, he's got the word on our little letter problem." The professor hung up the phone and started to dry his hair.

Looking the mirror, he noticed how long his hair had grown. Faith always suggested that he get his hair cut every month, as she didn't like the way he looked with long hair. "You have such a handsome face, there's no reason to cover it up," she had always said to him when she had noticed his hair getting longer.

After blow-drying his hair, the professor stepped into his bedroom to find clothes for what could be a long and interesting day.

*   *   *   *

Beads of sweat were dripping into his eyes. Dez swept them away with his sweatshirt sleeve as he continued his jog along the streets of Revmont. A girl wearing tight black stretchy pants and a white long-sleeve t-shirt smiled at him as he passed her.

He decided to jog without music on this Saturday morning. Dez was working up a good sweat when he turned past Nathan's grocery store on the right. His goal was to run five miles, and the grocery store was just over three from his apartment.

Dez realized that Nathan had the day off before looking for his car and stopped to catch his breath. He leaned against the wall of nearby building and wiped more sweat from his forehead.

He started to slowly jog as he made his way to the crosswalk near the street. Picking up his pace as the traffic light turned red, he ran across the street and felt that healthy burn in his calves. Dez was glad that was running again. All the beer that he had drank during the "dark ages" of the past couple months after the breakup had left love handles that he was determined to get rid of.

As he ran by the local barber shop and a roast beef joint, Dez recalled the times of last summer. A year ago around this time, he was trying to deal with being away from Koral for so long.

A long-distance relationship was something completely new and exciting for Dez; looking back on the entire length of the bond between Koral and himself, he realized that he'd never take part in one again.

It was tough for him to scrape together money to see Koral at times, especially last summer, as he was a freshly graduated college student with no career in sight. He could gaudily recall the first time flying out to see her; although Dez wasn't easily intimidated by anything, he was nervous about spending four days in Chicago with a family that he'd never met before.

Koral's mother and father adored Dez. He could remember the plushy hug that her mother had given him upon their first meeting. "Welcome to the family," she had said on that hot summer day. Koral's dog had softened up to him after only a few hours, and spent that night curled up with its owner and her boyfriend in bed.

Dez started to run faster, putting more strength behind his long strides along the sidewalk. His mind obsessed over memories of last summer. He recalled the see-through blue nightgown she had worn every night during the trip. He recollected the first meetings between him and her friends. Every single one of them loved his Boston accent.

The veins in Dez's neck were struggling to break through his skin as his running speed increased. He thought about the "private birthday party" that Koral had given him after getting home from a day-long visit to Navy Pier with her best friend Krystal and her fiancé.

Dez could intensely remember making love to Koral in her bed for the first time. She had wanted him to have sex with her on the floor so her parents wouldn't hear the bed creak. He could picture the way her breasts swayed from side to side as he entered her from behind on her floor.

Dez's face turned beat red as he passed by the park near his apartment. His muscles ached worse than he had ever felt in his life but his body wouldn't stop running. The memories from last summer fueled the inhabitance of pain within his bones.

The flood of memoria graced his mind after passing his apartment; he couldn't remove Koral's face from his mental vision. His legs finally gave out as he reached Revmont City Hall, which was a mile from his apartment. He collapsed onto a bench near a bus stop and let the bright sun beat down upon his tired body.

Dollops of sweat fell from his face as he unzipped his black sweatshirt, revealing a soaking wet blue "Friday the 13th" t-shirt underneath. An elderly man walking past stared at Dez as he walked by, his eyes glued to the sight of a man wearing a sweaty t-shirt with the face of a hockey-masked serial killer on the front.

Dez eased himself off the bench and stood up, stretching his arms in the middle of the sidewalk. He forgot all of the memories that had plagued his head for the past few minutes and took a look at Revmont life on a Saturday morning.

Dez was never up this early on a Saturday, he would normally be passed out in his bed still wearing his Red Sox cap after getting in at 5 a.m. after a long night of drinking with Chester and Johnny.

He looked around and started his walk back to the apartment. His legs were throbbing with pain. Walking up the stairs at home was a thorny task; it took nearly five minutes to walk up the single flight to his front door.

Dez dug through the pockets of the sweatshirt for his keys while leaning against the door. He found them and unlocked the door.

After limping through the kitchen, Dez hopped past his brother's room and subsided to the couch. Pain extruded from two locations in his body: his legs and his heart.

*   *   *   *

Professor Ulrich pulled into the Butterfield Building parking lot and turned off the car engine. He leaned over to the backseat and grabbed his aging leather bag.

He shoved his cell phone into the back pocket of his jeans and adjusted the bottom of his navy blue Whitesnake shirt to reveal a studded belt. The professor walked over to the building and ran up the staircase in an energized rush.

He avoided the elevator and jogged up the stairs. Coming around the corner of the third floor stairwell, he bumped into Professor Levin, who dropped a large stack of papers all over the ground.

"I'm so sorry, Amber," Professor Ulrich said as he leaned down to help the annoyed woman pick up her belongings. "I'm in a rush and I wasn't paying attention."

"It's fine, Bruce," Professor Levin replied. "Is everything okay? You don't seem yourself as of late." As she leaned over to help the professor pick up the papers, he caught a small glimpse of her breasts sticking out of a red bra.

"I'm doing alright," he said with a smile. "I've just been under a tremendous amount of extra stress lately." Professor Ulrich tried to organize the papers in his hand before she grabbed them.

"I'll fix them later," Professor Levin said with a snide look on her face. "I'm not teaching any classes until the third summer session, so if you need help with anything, please just ask." The unpleasant look vanished as her face lit up.

"Thanks, Amber, I'll let you know." She continued on her way down the stairs as the professor trotted up the last staircase to his floor.

Hurriedly unlocking his office door, he tossed his bag on the guest chair in front of him and picked up the phone. The professor dialed Clancy's number at the lab.

"Hey Clancy, it's Bruce, I'll be there in two minutes," he said, spurring all of the words together.

"Okay, Bruce," Clancy replied just before hanging up.

Professor Ulrich ran down the stairwell, this time slower as his anticipation grew for hearing Clancy's test results. He shoved the building's lobby door open and jogged across the campus to the nearby lab, located at the Valo Monstreun Building near NBU's admissions office.

Flinging the door open, he walked into the lobby and down into the basement of the building. Heading past the front desk of the lab, he caught a glance of Clancy sitting at a table next to a tower of blood samples.

The lab was small compared to other area colleges, but was ranked as one of New England's most efficient science departments in a popular college manual. Clancy was one of NBU's top forensics specialists, and had turned down a career teaching in England to spend time and live with his family in Boston.

Professor Ulrich greeted his colleague with a strong handshake. "It's nice to see you, Clancy," he said with a large smile. "I should come over to this building a little more often to see what you've been up to."

Clancy chuckled and removed his glasses. His rosy red cheeks glistened in the bright lights above the lab. "Believe me, it's always more exciting here than in that Butterfield Building of yours," he said with a laugh.

"So, what have you found?" Professor Ulrich wasted no time in questioning the results of Clancy's dating test on the letter. His eyes were staring directly into Clancy's.

After taking a deep breath, Clancy asked the professor to sit down. "Bruce, I honestly thought that the letter was some sort of joke. Zombies attacking people at a town square in 1882? You couldn't be serious at all."

The professor winced and looked away. Before he could say anything, Clancy held his hand up as to pause Professor Ulrich's words.

"Bruce, I ran the tests regardless of what I thought. Those two pieces of paper are 102 years old. They're the real deal. I was absolutely shocked." Clancy had a look of astonishment and disbelief. Suddenly, his Irish cheeks didn't present a quality of jolliness to the professor as they had normally did.

The professor couldn't speak. Hilda Benton's letter was real. Ignoring the possibility that she was lying in it, a grip of repulsion gripped his body.

"Clancy, thanks again, I have to go." The professor patted him on the shoulder, grabbed the manila envelope from the lab table and ran out of the room.

CHAPTER 11

▼

Opening his bedroom window, Dez let the cool air outside filter in his lungs. He scratched his chin and sighed. He was hoping for a good day; both his mind and his body needed it.

Johnny and Chester were dropping by the apartment at eight o'clock to begin the night out. It left him a few hours to relax and get ready. Dez had heard stories of Vincenzo's; it had the reputation of being the type of club where divorced and older women gathered to scope out younger guys who were only interested in tagging someone old enough to be their mother.

Dez had not been out with friends on a weekend night drinking and not thought about Koral. Loneliness and alcohol came hand-in-hand for him ever since the dissolution of their relationship.

What was he hoping for tonight? Attention was the first thing on Dez's mind. Attention from any female source, an older woman or not, would at least help his mind drift back into a normal realm of thinking. He hadn't had sex in nearly two months; the last person he was with was Koral.

Dez sighed again and figured that he would get started on readying himself for the night. Before walking into the bathroom, he heard Nathan's door open. His younger brother, looking disheveled, stepped out of the room wearing a black muscle t-shirt and blue jogging shorts.

"Why, hello beautiful," Dez sarcastically said to Nathan with a large smirk on his face,

"Oh, fuck you." Nathan flipped his brother the middle finger and walked into the kitchen, scraping his bare feet across the floor as if he had just learned how to walk.

Reaching into the refrigerator and grabbing the plastic carafe of orange juice, Nathan shot Dez a glare. "Hey, unemployed man over there, we really need to start grocery shopping on a weekly basis."

Dez shot him a glare back and said, "You're the breadwinner of this place. Plus, I'm old now, you should be supporting me." He laughed and gave his brother a playful punch to the arm.

Nathan forced a small grin and walked over to the cabinet to get a glass. He poured the remaining liquid in the bottle and began to sip it. Dez picked up the empty container, shook it, and tossed it into the wastebasket in the corner of the kitchen.

"What's the deal for tonight? I'm heading to a late movie with Lauren," said Nathan, finishing off the orange juice in his glass.

"We're going to this Vincenzo's place in Wallit. It's about a half hour away from here," Dez replied while searching through the kitchen for food. "I say you meet up with us around 3 or 4 in the morning somewhere."

"Hmm...Ryan's Diner cool with you?" Nathan placed the empty glass into the kitchen sink.

Dez nodded his head in agreement. "I'm sure I'll have no trouble convincing the boys to go. Johnny would eat there every single day if he had the money." He flipped back his bangs with his right hand and looked towards Nathan.

"Awesome. Give me a call as you guys are leaving the bar. I doubt Lauren will come, but I'll be there." Nathan burped and reached back into the fridge. "We really do need some food in here, Dez."

"Yes, I know." Dez sighed and pushed his brother to the side. "There's some Chinese food left over from last week in the back, bro. Look."

"Oh, I see it. Let me know what the deal is when you guys leave the bar, okay?" Nathan asked.

"You got it." Dez walked back towards his bedroom in hopes of finding something to wear for the night.

Dez's closet at one point had been decently organized, with t-shirts, dress shirts and jeans separated for easy location when he needed it. Koral was the one who usually cleaned it up for him. Every time she had come to visit him, she had complained that Dez had destroyed the system she created for him the last time she was there.

Sometimes it was hard for him to wear certain clothes that Koral had always said looked good on him. Dez grabbed a black Calvin Klein button-down shirt and threw it in the bed. He then thought of how she had said that the shirt had made his arms looked amazing. Dez quickly grabbed the shirt and threw it in the back of the closet.

I can't keep doing this to myself, he thought to himself as he struggled to find a neutral piece of clothing that would not invoke any romantic memories for him. Dez passed by what was a majority of black-colored shirts before finally settling his mind on the original shirt he had picked out.

Dez grabbed a pair of green-tinted stressed jeans from the floor of his bedroom and tossed them beside the shirt he had just selected out on his bed.

He walked into the bathroom and searched for his razor. After peering in the mirror, he noticed considerable growth gathering on his chin. After smearing shaving cream on his face, he began to swipe at the hair.

Dez looked deep into the mirror and focused on his eyes. "I look so fucking strained," he said aloud.

＊　　　＊　　　＊　　　＊

"What makes this situation really ironic is that you know that no one would ever believe us," Professor Ulrich said in between sips of a diet soda.

Dane removed his eyesight from the ass of a student walking past the Butterfield Building and nodded his head. "I know, Professor. We don't have very many options here."

The professor adjusted his black sunglasses and took another sip of his drink. "I'm really lucky that you're just as scientifically insane as I am, or else I would have been in more trouble that I am now." He looked over at Dane, even though his eyes were shielded by the black plastic.

Dane smiled and looked directly at his reflection in the professor's sunglasses. "Who else would actually think that a simple yet rare eclipse in space could cause the dead to rise from their graves? Any other assistant that you would have had would have completely laughed in your face, Professor Ulrich."

The professor grinned and turned away. "Now we have the question of just what the hell we're going to do. We're absolutely stuck here, Dane. Either it's our own sick minds working overtime on this whole thing, or come the morning hours of tomorrow, we're going to be kicking ourselves that we have even worried about it in the first place."

Dane nodded in agreement. "We just have to keep in touch tonight. If anything does happen, we'll need to meet up immediately. What are you going to do tonight? Just hang around your place?"

"This may sound ridiculous, but I'm really worried about my ex-wife." The professor winced as the words came out of his mouth. A girl wearing a tight purple shirt and jeans walked past the staircase and smiled at him. Professor Ulrich returned the smile and stretched his back. "If there really is going to be danger tonight, I want to make sure she's safe."

Dane sneezed and wiped his nose. "That's completely understandable, Professor. You guys *were* married, after all. Even though I've never had a relationship on that level, I would figure that even after a divorce there's still some feelings of care on each side."

Professor Ulrich finished the remaining drops in his can of soda and placed it on the stair in front of him. "Do me a favor and never get married, buddy. You're much better off." The professor flicked an ant that was crawling near his foot, then cleared his throat. "I still want to make sure nothing happens to her."

Dane began to stand up and threw his messenger bag over his shoulder. "Well, I need to get moving. I'm not going to tell my friends about the transit, but I'd still like to be with some other people, just in case something *does* happen."

"Dane, I haven't said this yet, but…thank you for helping me out with this whole thing. It takes someone with a real sense of science, not to mention ambition in the field, to even pay the slightest amount of attention to something like this." The professor removed his sunglasses to reveal a look of genuine appreciation.

Dane gave the professor a firm handshake. "I'm here, Professor."

"Be careful tonight," said Professor Ulrich as he got up and stretched his arms. "I'll be in touch with you."

Dane walked down the staircase and into the parking lot. The professor watched as his graduate assistant faded off into the sunset, which was slowly allowing the evening sky to embrace the city.

Professor Ulrich put his sunglasses back on and leaned against the building's lobby door. Reaching into his leather bag, he pulled out his cell phone and flipped it open. Oh Bruce, what are you doing, he asked himself in his mind.

Flipping through his phonebook, he scrolled down until he found Faith's cell phone number. "Let's get this over with," he said to himself aloud.

After hitting the "send" button the phone, the professor brought the object up to his head. A few rings later, he heard Faith's voice on the other line.

"Bruce?" the faint female voice said. It sounded as if she had either just woken up, or better yet, hesitant to answer the phone at all.

"Faith, listen to me. Where are you going to be tonight?" The professor seemed stern and serious.

"Bruce, you can't play games with me like this. I was merely trying to open the lines of communication with you, and you belligerently rejected my attempts to do so." The concern in her voice was creeping its way into the professor's mind as he began to frown.

"I'm sorry for blowing up at you earlier in the week. I'm just under a lot of stress, Faith. Just please listen to me," said the professor.

"You were *always* under a lot of stress." Faith's voice started to sound more full.

"Listen to me. Where are you going to be tonight?" The professor had dropped his bag to the ground and was kneeling on the ground. The volume was of his voice had steadily increased.

"I'm just going to Vincenzo's with some of the women from work. Did you think I had a date or something? I really don't understand you sometimes, Bruce. I really don't."

"That's not the issue. I just want to know where you are, I have a bad feeling about tonight. I can't get into it, it's just this feeling that I have." Professor Ulrich felt a moment of ease become lifted out of his mind. "That's the place in Wallit, right?"

Faith sighed and breathed into the phone. "Yeah, it's right off Interstate-93. I guess if you want to stop by, it's fine."

The professor smiled, but it quickly vanished. "Well, then, I'll see you there." He reached for his leather bag, draped it across his shoulders, and walked down the staircase.

The sun was making its way into the ground on the horizon, leaving room for the night sky.

CHAPTER 12

▼

The bottom button on his black shirt was left unbuttoned. Dez had always left it open, just so a small view of his studded belt would be showing.

He looked at himself in the bathroom mirror. Even though he thought he looked attractive and ready for a night out with the guys, there was something missing from the sight in the mirror. It was almost as if Koral's bright dyed red hair should be glistening in the reflection, completing the picture of Dez.

With a groan, he shook his head and flung the vision out of his mind. Dez reached for the yellow tube of hair glue and squeezed a generous amount onto his palm. With a slow motion, he filtered the sticky substance in his black hair. After toweling areas of his hair, Dez decided that he looked like he should be fronting a rock band. There was something satisfying about that look, he thought.

Nathan popped his head into the bathroom. "Hey, Jon Bon Jovi said you have to pay him royalties if you're going to wear your hair like that," he said with a laugh.

Dez's genuine smile reflected back across to him in the mirror. "Oh, thanks for the support. I'm sure of these older women tonight are going to dig me. If not, I'll just get trashed and eat some pancakes with you later." The smile was strongly smug across his face.

Nathan jumped on Dez and punched him in the arm. "I'm going in a few minutes. So, you'll call me when you're leaving the bar?" He adjusted the white t-shirt under his blue polo shirt.

"As soon as we head out of there, I'll give you a buzz," Dez said while fixing the sides of his hair.

"Sweet. Later bro." Nathan grabbed his Red Sox hat off of the kitchen table, placed his cell phone in his pocket and left the apartment.

Dez heard the door slam as he turned off the bathroom light. He glanced at the clock in the living room. Chester and Johnny would be arriving shortly. He headed into the kitchen and reached for a beer in the refrigerator. Twisting off the cap and throwing it into the barrel, he took a seat on the living room couch.

After a few moments, Dez got up and turned on the stereo near the television set. He scrolled over to the third CD in the deck and hit the "shuffle" button. The sounds of the Deftones filled the room as "Anniversary of an Uninteresting Event" and its haunting piano melody caroused the mind of Dez.

He sat back down on the couch and took a gulp of the beer in his hand. Staring into the night sky through the living room window, Dez thought of Koral. He thought of her soft hair easing itself on his chest. He thought of her wet kiss on his full lips.

Dez thought of how much he loved her, of how much she completed his persona. His eyes began to water as he recalled all of the moments he work up next to her, certain that she was the person he'd spend the rest of his life with. The tears began to take shape in his eyes.

The cold liquid funneled its way down his throat as he drifted into the realm of memories. Just two months ago, he was in Koral's room, grasping her body close to his as they both lied in bed. He would have never imagined that she would have completely destroyed him following that fateful final journey to the Midwest.

Dez snapped back into reality when his cell phone rang. He wiped his eyes, took a sip of beer and walked over to his bedroom to pick up the phone.

"Hey, it's Chester, we'll be there in a few." Chester sounded as if he were ready to scream at a football game for three hours.

"Sounds good, bro. See you soon." Dez hung up the phone and wiped his eyes again. He couldn't be doing this, he thought. Like Chester had always told him, things happen for a reason, even if he didn't truly quite understand why yet.

Dez wanted to move on. He wanted to be able to wake up one day and have that sick feeling inside of his chest be gone forever from his body. Koral meant too much to him, though. Even at his young age, Dez had honestly believed that he had found the one girl for him, the one that would make him happy for the rest of his days. Dez thought he had truly found his soulmate.

It was all gone now. Dez had sometimes felt that there was no reason to live without Koral; his life was nothing but a misconstrued and chaotic mess without the one person who not only kept him grounded, but also happy.

Dez checked his eyes in the bathroom mirror to make sure that they were not red anymore. After putting some cologne on, he finished off his beer and put the empty bottle into the sink. He unlocked the apartment door and opened it slightly. The cool breeze from outside started to leak into the hallway.

The Deftones album playing in the living room had ended, allowing U2's *The Joshua Tree* album to begin to play. Dez lowered the volume as "Where The Streets Have No Name" kicked in.

Dez heard a car door slam outside and walked over to the open door in the hallway. Chester and Johnny got out of the car and began to make their way up the staircase. "Peek-a-boo dude," Johnny said with a devious look on his face. He was wearing skintight black jeans and a New York Dolls t-shirt that had been kept together on the signs with safety pins.

Chester filed into the apartment first. He had ditched his normal use of a cow-boy hat to let his brown wavy hair show.

"This Vincenzo's place won't know what hit 'em after we leave. The *women* there won't know what hit 'em!" Chester screamed in the hallway. The look on his face was a devious match to Johnny's.

Dez felt his depressed emotions fade away as the prospective excitement of the night sunk in. "Oh boy. I'm guessing this night is going to be somewhat memo-rable." He gave Chester a pat on the shoulder and looked towards Johnny. "Then again, we always say that every time we go out to a new bar."

"This is true." Johnny was fumbling through some of the CDs in the living room. "Hey, we can pre-game here before we head out?"

Dez reached into the fridge and grabbed a beer for his friend. He tossed it to Johnny, who was looking at the back of a CD after turning on the television. He left the channel on CNN to catch the score of the afternoon's Red Sox game.

Those on the Eastern half of the United States will have the opportunity to view the transit, which is expected to begin around 1 a.m. tomorrow morning. Astronomers and stargazers alike are thrilled with the chance to view such a rare event.

"Fuck, I just wanted to find out the score of the game. Hey Dez, have you seen this shit about Venus?" Johnny had his feet up on the glass coffee table.

"Yeah, there's been some coverage in the news about that lately. We'll proba-bly get a chance to see that after we leave the bar." Dez was looking for his black Doc Marten boots in his bedroom. "Dude, that was on TV the last time you were here."

This rare transit, lasting just over six hours and 12 minutes, will showcase Venus' trek across the night sky. Those in the viewing area will see the illustrious planet climb near the sun's right limb as a small, black, sharp-edged dark dot.

The newscaster wrapped up the coverage of the transit just as the MLB scores were showing across the bottom of the screen. "Awesome!" Johnny shouted from the living room. "I knew that Arroyo would pitch a good game. I wonder who hit home runs this afternoon."

Chester opened a bag of chips in the kitchen and walked into the living room to sit down. "I totally want to see this Venus thing. Too bad I'll probably be the only sober one that'll appreciate it. As a matter of fact, I'll be the *only* one sober tonight," he said in between crunching handfuls of potato chips.

Dez walked in holding his boots in his hand. Sitting on the recliner in the corner, he reached down to slip his feet into them and tie them. "Let's get the hell out of here," he said after adjusting the laces on his boots.

"Giddy up," said Chester while cramming a final handful of chips into his mouth. Johnny headed into the bathroom to check his hair.

Locking the door behind them, Dez felt the cold air push his hair ajar. He could not believe that just over a year ago, he would have been walking to Chester's car while holding Koral's hand, eagerly anticipating an evening where they both would get drunk and end up making out in the back of the car on the way home.

Although he had been friends with Chester and Johnny for well over a decade, it felt out of place nowadays to go out with them and not talk about how he and Koral were doing, or having her call and Dez passing the phone around so she could say hi to everyone.

Dez opened the right backseat door and slipped onto the cushion. He tried not to kick the half-empty bottles of water on the floor of Chester's car.

Chester adjusted the rear view mirror and started the engine to his car. Johnny was fumbling with the radio, trying to find a suitable radio station. Chester's 2001 Ford Taurus drove smoothly, something Dez wished his Jeep would do.

As the group pulled out of the driveway to the apartment, Dez placed his head against the door window and closed his eyes. *It'll all come together soon, Dez.* The voice in the back of his head was trying to reassure him of the future, of a time where thoughts of Koral would be miniscule and irrelevant.

Just have some fun tonight, Dez. The voice was clear. Dez opened his eyes and watched the stars shine brightly in the night sky.

*   *   *   *

He dropped the fourth gray hair into the sink and turned on the faucet. The professor, by all rights, should have been mostly gray-haired by this age, however, he had only found a few stray hairs in his otherwise brown locks.

In one sense, Professor Ulrich could not believe he was actually getting ready for a night out with his ex-wife. Furthermore, he was in disbelief that the transit was a matter of hours away.

The professor settled on black stretch pants and a tight red t-shirt. He picked out one of his several black suit jackets to along with the outfit. He could almost predict that tonight of all nights, he would probably be approached by more women than he could imagine.

Letting his brown hair spike its way into different directions, he pulled the red shirt over his head and onto his torso. The stretch pants were a little snug in the waist; the professor figured he had gained a little weight over the course of the divorce.

Looking at himself in the tall mirror in his bedroom, the professor took a deep breath and collected his thoughts. He stepped back and sat down on his bed, letting the mattress sink in with his body.

"What am I in store for tonight?" he asked himself aloud. Seeing Faith after the divorce had always taken its toll on the professor's mind. To this day, it still felt like she broke the marriage in half because of her own inability to feel loved and be comfortable with a man.

His mind shifted gears as his eyes caught part of the moonlight that was trying to force its way in through the bedroom window. He thought of Hilda's letter and the vivid detail of the horror her and her father were exposed to the last time the Venus transit had occurred. The professor pictured Faith and himself in the same situation.

With that thought, he now realized exactly why he was going to see Faith tonight. He still cared about her. There was no way that the possibility of chaos harming her would be allowed by Professor Ulrich. There was a significant chunk of his heart that will always belong to her, regardless of the pain that she caused him over the past year.

He stood up and walked over to his dresser, picking up the cologne bottle and dabbing some of it on his neck and wrists. The professor reached for his black suit jacket and made his way into the kitchen. He poured himself a glass of iced tea and leaned against the counter while taking small sips of it. It was already past 10 p.m., and he figured that Faith was probably already at Vincenzo's.

Professor Ulrich could picture his ex-wife sitting at the bar, drinking a sour apple martini and laughing with her chest out, revealing the top part of her tanned breasts. Other men would consistently gawk at her whenever he was with her during their relationship, and although it never bothered him before, his skin crawled with irritation whenever he pictured the post-divorce Faith being checked out.

The professor put on his suit jacket and walked into the bathroom. He looked over himself in the mirror, making sure he looked somewhat decent.

Tension filled his bones; the night that lied ahead was unpredictable and vague. The possibility of absolute destruction and dismay during the transit coupled with seeing his ex-wife was a hard load to handle for the professor. Part of him wanted to undress, put on sweatpants and spend the rest of the evening watching movies on the couch.

Professor Ulrich was not a coward, and he refused to take the easy route out of anything. This was evident in his battles with Faith when their marriage first became rocky. He fought and fought for the good of the marriage, but in the end it was all for nothing. He was starting to believe that it was never meant to be.

The professor recollected himself and shook out the feelings of apprehension. He grabbed his keys, cell phone and wallet and headed out of the apartment, locking the door behind him. The loud crash of the door rang through his ears.

Before stepping into his car, he drew his head back and looked up into the stars of the bright Boston sky. Professor Ulrich was prepared for the worst, he realized. It was almost as if fate had drawn this evening out for him.

He opened the door of the car and sat in the driver's seat. It was time to go.

CHAPTER 13

▼

Chester stepped on the gas pedal as he merged onto the highway, nearly cutting off an old blue pickup truck in the process. "Hey, fuck you buddy!" screamed Chester out the window at the driver of the truck after honking his horn.

"It's such a warm and welcoming city to drive in, don't you guys think?" Johnny asked sarcastically. He grinned and turned to the backseat to look at Dez, who had his focus on a car two lanes over that had a redhead behind the steering wheel.

"Oh, come on buddy! You're not going to be looking for the 43-year-old version of Koral tonight, are you?" Johnny said, throwing his hands up in the air.

Dez smiled and shook his head in disagreement. "Absolutely not. Hey, if there's some 43-year-old chick that digs my style, I am very much going to take advantage of that." Dez forced out the fib in hopes of quieting his friend.

The truth was that Dez's thoughts were completely swimming in the realm of Koral. He had faced the notion that there was no escape from thinking about her. Even if was with another woman, it would be rough for his mind to turn all of the attention away from the heartbreak he had experienced.

Johnny rolled down the window, sending a rush of cool air throughout the car. Dez's bangs started to sway back and forth. He brushed them off to the side with his hand and allowed his head to lean back in his seat.

Dez wondered what Koral was doing right this second as his sight veered off into the night. Was she with another guy? Was she on a date? Was she at home, scrap booking pictures of some sort of event that she had attended in the past couple months?

The questions plagued his mind constantly. The worst thoughts of her engaging in sexual activity with other men drove his heart into a violent stir. Dez could not stomach the thought of her beautiful naked body in the bed of someone else.

"Snap out of it, bro," Chester shouted, turning around quickly look at his friend while switching lanes on the highway. "Don't you dare give us that depressed look the entire night."

Dez laughed and lost focus of his paranoia. "I promise I'll smile the entire night, Chester." Another lie took form.

*   *   *   *

The windows were down in Professor Ulrich's car, allowing him to feel the touch of the air outside. Confusion ran rampant within his mind; there was no set way that the following evening would unfold.

He flipped his directional and quickly switched lanes. There were very few cars on the road, odd for a typical weekend night outside of Boston. The breeze was getting stronger as the professor felt a chill run up and down his body.

He let his hands grip the steering wheel tighter as the urge to see Faith grew stronger and stronger. Professor Ulrich flipped on the radio dial. "Dead Souls," his favorite Joy Division song, was being covered by Nine Inch Nails on one of Boston's smaller rock radio stations.

Suddenly, his mind escaped back to nearly two years ago. He could recall being in a gothic/new wave-esque club with Faith, holding her hand tightly while ordering a Midori sour at the bar.

Those times were so much more jovial for Professor Ulrich. Everything seemed to be going well for him: he was enjoying his time at NBU and he had a beautiful woman by his side. But now, those times were over, and were a mere shadow of how the professor used to live his life.

On this June night, he wished he could go back to those times.

CHAPTER 14

▼

Dez rolled up his window as his group's destination approached. Passing by a round of small bars and clubs, in addition to fast-food joints, was Vincenzo's.

Pulling into the parking lot, Johnny's eye caught a group of five women, all looking old enough to be his mother, entering the club. "I'm guessing we're going to have a very atypical evening. What do you say, fellas?"

Chester winked at his friend while looking for an available parking space. He found a spot next to an older Monte Carlo that had four older women sitting in it, all smoking cigarettes with the windows down.

Turning off the engine, Chester looked into the rear view mirror to see Dez looking away from the women. "Hey buddy, what did I tell you about that depressed look?" Looking over at Chester, Dez smiled and opened the car door.

Walking over to their car, Chester leaned into the backseat window to face two of the four women in the vehicle. A blonde that clearly had some major plastic surgery done to her face smiled at the young man. "How are you ladies doing tonight?"

The brunette sitting next to the blonde, showing a generous amount of cleavage in her tight black tank top, blew smoke out of the corner of her mouth. "We're doing fine, honey. May I ask what you and your playmates are doing here this evening?"

"Ouch." Chester grinned and looked away. Johnny patted him on the back and motioned for the group to head into Vincenzo's. "Well, I guess we'll see you ladies in there, then."

Dez could hear one of the women saying "Sure thing sweetie!" as he looked back at them while walking towards the entrance to the club. "What the hell are we doing here?" he questioned to himself aloud.

"I don't see Betty's car anywhere. I forgot to ask her if she was coming here tonight." Chester was peering away from the club and surveying the loads of cars in the opposite side of the parking lot. "I should have called her before we left."

"Is that the slamming nurse babe that always busts your balls?" Johnny asked.

"Yeah, she's really cool. She laughed a few days ago when I told her that we were all planning on coming here." Chester had a childish grin on his face while giggling.

"Oh, I wonder why? Is it because this place was designed for people going through a midlife crisis?" Dez's harsh look reinforced his statement.

"You're just *bitter*. Cheer the fuck up and have a few drinks. Maybe you'll find a sugar momma tonight, Dez." Chester had draped his right arm around Dez's shoulders. "God knows we all could use one of those."

Dez forced a small smile and continued walking to the entrance. A "Vincenzo's" sign was lit up with orange neon lights. The building itself looked somewhat run-down on the outside, fitting in perfectly with the nature of the surrounding businesses. It seemed like this district was meant for nightlife.

The bouncer at the door looked like he was in his fifties. His buzz cut revealed a short mass of gray hair, offset by his bulging biceps.

Chester was the first to enter the club. He pulled out his driver's license and handed it to the large man in front of him. The bouncer looked it over, bent it slightly and glanced at Chester's face. He handed the card back to him as Johnny handed over his.

After looking over the ID, Dez pulled out his from the back pocket of his jeans. The photo on his driver's license had always sent Koral into laughter, he could remember. She had always said that he looked a lot more "tough" because of the mean look on his face.

Dez sighed as gave the bouncer the ID. Within 20 seconds, the man handed it back to him.

"Well, are you boys ready?" Chester asked the group as he pulled open the door to the club. Johnny walked in first, followed by Dez, who was trying to adjust the white t-shirt underneath his collared black dress shirt.

Dez swiped his bangs out of his face and stood in the lobby of the club. He immediately noticed that he and his friends were the youngest patrons in the entire bar. He looked over to Chester, who had a gigantic smile on his face.

Johnny was already checking out a punky older woman who had green streaks running through her hair.

Chester felt the itch that normally encompassed him at a few points throughout the day. He knew he had to be careful of the Vincenzo's security team investigating anything suspicious in the bathroom. He hated snorting meth in public places, for fear of getting busted. However, the urge was just too strong for him to overcome. Chester immediately realized that he should have cooked his fix in the car before the group headed into the club.

"Guys, I'll be right back," Chester said while casually walking over to the men's bathroom. Dez and Johnny headed over to one of the two bars in the club.

Leaning over the counter next to a very attractive blonde-haired woman, Dez raised his hand to retrieve the bartender's attention. The woman caught wind of him and looked at over at Dez. "You smell good, cutie," she said with a wink.

Dez resisted the urge to blush and winked back at the woman. The bartender caught a glimpse of Dez's hand and finished pouring a drink for a woman towards the end of the bar. He walked over to Dez and asked him what he could get him.

"I'll take a Guinness," he replied. Looking over at Johnny, Dez said, "And he'll have a gin and tonic."

"Sure thing." The bartender reached to the roof of the bar stand to fetch two glasses. As Dez surveyed the entire dance floor, he noticed that the woman sitting next to him was now staring at his body. He tried to ignore it.

"So, what brings someone so young to a place like this?" the blonde asked Dez. "Someone so cute should be in downtown Boston picking up college chicks." Her conniving beam was frozen on her face.

"My friend wanted to check this place out." Dez caught himself peering down at the woman's breasts. "He's a tad adventurous."

"Well, anytime you guys feel like it, me and my friends will be sitting right here." She lightly licked her lips. "Please don't *disappoint* me, cutie."

The bartender slid over the dark beer and the gin and tonic. "That'll be $11.50, buddy."

Dez reached into his back pocket and pulled a ten and three dollar bills. Folding them up, he handed them to the bartender. Before handing Johnny's drink to him, he smiled at the flirty woman.

"Thanks, dude," Johnny said as his friend handed him the drink. Dez wiped off the stickiness from the glass on his jeans and took a small sip of his beer. Looking around, he saw Chester walking out of the bathroom.

"Why, how grand is this? My friends are *already* drinking." His eyes were glazed over and he was scratching his left cheek. "Have you guys seen some of the honies at this place?"

Dez laughed and rolled his eyes. "Well, this will be an interesting night."

*   *   *   *

Fixing his hair in the reflection of the car window, the professor took a deep breath and lets his chest expand.

He adjusted the white and red U2 pin on his black suit jacket and began to look around the parking lot for Faith's car. Professor Ulrich finally caught the sight of the red 2002 Grand Prix parked near the front entrance of Vincenzo's.

Walking past it, he stopped for a minute to glance inside of the car. A pink sweater was strewn across the backseat, along with a few empty bottles of diet soda and various fitness magazines. The professor could not remember whether or not she owned the sweater during their relationship.

The bright orange neon sign blaring in the front of the club, Professor Ulrich reached into his inside jacket pocket for his wallet to find his driver's license. After handing it to the bouncer, he checked the time on his cell phone.

"Here you go, man. Have a good night." The bouncer smiled and handed back the ID.

"Thanks, you too." The professor returned the smile and pulled open the door to the club. Walking in, he instantaneously began to look for Faith's blonde hair.

Heading over to the bar, he noticed a younger group of guys that looked like college students. One of them resembled someone who wished he was a rock star, and one of the others might have been stuck in the punk movement of 1977.

Walking past a group of women sitting at the bar, he saw Faith on the opposite side of the club. He could barely make out her tight black pants. Her blonde hair was straightened, revealing very little of her dark brown roots.

Professor Ulrich closed and his eyes and mustered the courage to walk over to his ex-wife.

CHAPTER 15

▼

Depeche Mode's "Enjoy The Silence" was playing loudly as Professor Ulrich began his walk over to Faith. As he drew closer to her, he noticed the tribal tattoo on the small of her back. There was no doubt in his mind; she was just as beautiful as when they were together.

He could hear her laugh, a cute and quirky giggle that the professor had always loved. He tried not to sneak up behind her, however, he let his arms grace her shoulders while letting out a small "hello."

Faith jumped out of her seat and closed her eyes. The professor's touch was an immediate recognition for her. She placed her right hand on top of one of his and turned her entire body around.

"Hi, Bruce," she said with a faint smile.

"Hi Faith, how are you?" Professor Ulrich's hand was gently placed on her side. For a moment, touching her felt right.

"I'm fine. How long have you been here?" she questioned. Faith brushed away her ex-husband's hand and picked up her drink. It was a sour apple martini.

The professor motioned to the bartender and turned to Faith. "I just got here a few minutes ago."

"I like that shirt." Faith was reaching into the professor's suit jacket to feel the material of the red shirt.

"I'll have a Bud Light, and another of whatever she's having," Professor Ulrich said to the bartender while pointing at Faith's empty martini glass. The bartender nodded and walked away.

Leaning against the side of the bar, Professor Ulrich surveyed the area surrounding he and Faith. "This place seems pretty decent. Have you been coming here often?"

She nodded and smiled at him. "It's a nice place. All the people from my office love coming here on the weekend." The bartender handed her the sour apple martini and twisted off the cap to the professor's bottle of beer.

After grabbing the beer from the bartender's hand, he motioned to Faith. "Let's take a walk." Faith tapped her friend on the shoulder, a woman barely into her forties, wearing a blue tank top and too much makeup.

"I'll be back in a few," she said to the friend while picking up both the napkin and her drink.

Professor Ulrich took a long sip of his drink and began to walk away from the bar with Faith trailing right behind him.

"Faith, listen to me for a few minutes. Some of what I'm going to tell you may seem a bit crazy." The look on his face was one that was looking for sympathy. His eyes were peering directly into Faith's. When she looked away and rolled her eyes, the professor noticed glitter garnering the cleavage of her tight black tank top.

"There's a reason why I was so concerned with where you were going to be tonight." The professor did not care how much he had raised his voice. "I was born a scientist, Faith. It's in my nature to question the validity of most things in life. However, there's one thing that has got me in shambles."

"And what's that, Bruce? The fact that you can accept simple communication with your ex-wife?" Her eyes were hardened and direct.

Professor Ulrich winced in emotional pain and looked away, trying to keep his composure. "Our relationship has nothing to do with the fact that tonight's Venus transit is going to cause destruction here on Earth."

"Have you completely lost your fucking mind? Or have you been staying up late watching sci-fi movies for the past week?" Faith's right hand was on her hip, while the other tightly gripped the bottom of the martini glass.

"Calm down, Faith. Listen to me." The professor was finding it hard to convey the pure terror in which he believed was going to happen when Venus, the Earth and the sun aligned later in the night. "I found a document dating back to the last time this transit happened in 1882. It caused the dead to rise in Revmont, Faith. I read the letter written by a little girl who was trapped in a shop while creatures tore apart the town."

Faith's eyes twinkled in the green and yellow lights of the dance floor a few feet away. She took a sip of her martini and shook her head. "You have got to be kidding me, Bruce. You have really lost it."

Professor Ulrich placed his beer down on a nearby table. Grabbing Faith's sides with both hands, he pulled her closer to him and stared directly into her bright blue eyes. "I'm not fucking around, Faith. I want you to be safe. I have no idea if this transit is going to cause frenzied effects anywhere else in the area…or the world, for that matter."

Before Faith could speak, the professor squeezed her sides tight. "I just want to make sure that whatever happens tonight, you're safe. Did you have plans for later with your friends from work?"

"Jesus, Bruce. I wanted to go to Ryan's Diner in Revmont, but none of them were interested." Faith pouted her lips and looked down.

Instantly, a wave of memories encompassed Professor Ulrich's mind and body. Ryan's Diner was a 24-hour restaurant in Revmont that he and Faith would eat at after a night out in Boston while they were still together.

A flash of light lit up the professor's mind. He suddenly could see himself sitting in a booth at the diner with Faith, laughing and looking into her gorgeous face. They would head to Ryan's Diner after hitting a round of bars in Boston. Professor Ulrich loved seeing Faith drunk; she would flirt with him and rub his crotch area, stating she was horny.

As he recalled the memories of being at the diner, Faith snapped him back into conscious reality. "Bruce? Do you want to go to Ryan's Diner after we leave here?" She was looking up at him without a smile.

Professor Ulrich spaced out for a moment. "Sure." He promptly thought of how the rest of the night would pan out. "The transit starts a little after 1 a.m. Is it okay to leave then?" The professor felt an instant of calm overtake his body.

"That's fine. I still don't believe your chaos theory, though. But at least I'll be able to get a good meal out of it." Faith smiled and grabbed the professor's arm. "Now, let's go back to my friends so they don't think we ditched them and got remarried," she said with a laugh.

Professor Ulrich forced a smile and playfully shoved his ex-wife. Even thought the discomfort in his stomach was ever-growing with uncertainty, he at least felt relieved that Faith would be with him for the rest of the evening.

CHAPTER 16

▼

Dez's eyes followed the bounce of a black-haired pale woman's buttocks on the dance floor from the bar. Wearing a sparkly silver skirt cut just above the knees, she swayed up and down and back and forth to the rhythm of the Berlin song playing loudly.

Attention was broken when Johnny walked past him, holding a beer in each hand and laughing. A little over an hour had passed, and already his friend was blasted. It looked as though Johnny was flirting with the same punk rocker-looking woman he had eyed the minute the group walked into Vincenzo's.

Dez looked down and shook the half-empty bottle of Bud Light in his left hand. It was his fourth, and slowly the evening was sinking into a typical post-Koral weekend. Most parts of his mind wanted to curl up in bed and shut off the outside world.

He ignored the pumping volume of the club's music and leaned back onto the bar. Taking a long sip of his drink, his eyes were once again fixated on the woman on the dance floor. She had looked no more than forty, Dez thought to himself. She also looked as if she still had a grasp on popular culture.

Dez contemplated approaching her, but quickly dropped the thought as the realization of his self-esteem kicked into his mind. Koral had done a number on his confidence; it was going to take a significant amount of time for him to repair himself in that area.

Peering off to his left, Chester was easing in and out of consciousness. His head would occasionally bob back up when Dez poked him in the side. Chester had taken too much of a hit, Dez thought to himself.

Dez wished he could be like his two friends. They both had no worries in the world, it seemed, and heartbreak had almost no effect on either. In the grand scheme of their friendship, he appreciated the consistent advice given to him by the two. However, it still wasn't helping the revolting crack in the middle of his heart to heal.

He watched on as Johnny planted his lips on the woman with green streaks through her dark hair. Dez smiled and thought of how he was probably a little greater than half of that woman's age.

Johnny could be overheard screaming over the music, asking the woman if she remembered being alive when The Clash was still together.

Dez finished off the remnants of beer in the bottle and gently placed it on the bar. He motioned to the bartender to give him another. Reaching into his pocket to pull out a five-dollar bill, he stared at the object of his attention on the dance floor.

As Dez uncrumpled the bill, he noticed out of the corner of his eye that the pale woman he was leering at was heading in his general direction. He nudged Chester, who gave him a look of disgust and said, "What?"

"Forget it, dude. Go back to fucking sleep." Dez turned his head away and handed the bartender the money. Picking up the bottle of beer, he gulped it and looked at the clock on the wall of the club.

"Bartender?" The woman was sitting right next to Dez on the stool beside him. "I'll take a white Russian, please."

With the mouth of the bottle barely on his bottom lip, he nonchalantly attempted to look her at face. What he noticed were black-painted fingernails holding a ten-dollar bill. Dez loved women who painted their fingernails black.

She was wearing a low-cut red shirt with a black star pattern gracing most of the front. Dez figured that her breasts were at least a C cup. Her blue-green eyes were staring directly ahead at the line of liquor bottles on the shelves on the wall. The woman's face was oval-shaped and pale.

"Thank you," the woman said as she was handed her drink. Her voice was of a quaint nature, solidifying beauty to Dez's ears.

Taking a sip from her drink, the woman's eyes surveyed the opposite side of the bar. Wiping a bead of sweat from her brow, she leaned back for the bar stool and sat down. Crossing her milky white legs, she placed her drink on the bar and looked over at Dez.

Dez tried to hide his line of vision, attempting to pretend as if he was looking at the label on his bottle of beer. Out of the corner of his eye, he could see that the woman was looking directly at him with a smile on her face.

"I like your shirt," she said, placing a hand on Dez's chest to feel the material. Dez tried his hardest to refrain from blushing.

"Thanks." Dez flashed a toothy grin at the woman, who had inched over to him. "That's an interesting design pattern on your blouse."

"Thank you, sweetie." Her chest graced the small amount of open between her and Dez. "Tell me something, cutie. Why is it that a baby-face like yourself might be in a place with nothing but us over-the-hill women?"

Dez laughed and shook his head, then took a gulp of his drink. "I'm with a few friends. They were interested in checking this place out." He tried not to stare at her cleavage.

"Well, I can safely say that you're just about the best looking guy in here." Her dimples hid her age, which Dez might have guessed was not even forty years old.

Dez finally let his cheeks turn red as he leaned in for conversation with the woman. "That's very sweet of you to say. My name's Dez."

The woman smiled and extended her right hand. "Hi Dez, I'm Hannah."

*   *   *   *

Wiping his hands with a few pieces of rough brown paper, the professor looked at his face in the bathroom mirror and analyzed his hair. Shaping a side lock that was out of place, he sighed and exited the bathroom.

He could hear a rock song from the late '70s playing loudly as he turned the corner out of the bathroom's hallway, but couldn't place the band in his head. Professor Ulrich reached into his pocket for money and walked over to the opposite bar from where Faith was sitting.

The professor caught an open spot at the crowded bar and leaned against it before motioning for the bartender. A five-dollar bill in his hand, he ordered a beer and slipped the money to the bartender. Next to him, he could overhear two people talking about their favorite Motley Crue songs.

"You're not even old to have seen them in their heyday," the woman told what looked to be a rocker-type guy with jet black hair, who Professor Ulrich thought to be half the woman's age. "I was just getting out of high school when I saw them on the *Shout At The Devil* tour."

"That's fucking incredible," the man replied. "I always wished that I could have been old enough to have seen all of those bands when they were huge."

The rocker suddenly became fixated on Professor Ulrich's chest as the bartender handed him his beer. "Hey, that's an awesome pin! Are you a big fan?" the man asked the professor.

It took the professor a moment before he realized what the black-haired kid was talking about. He had almost forgotten that he had thrown on his vintage U2 pin onto his black suit jacket before heading out to the club.

"I'm a huge fan, I've seen them nearly 15 times." Professor Ulrich nodded to the kid and raised his beer bottle. "The name's Professor Bruce Ulrich. How's it going?" He gave the rocker a firm handshake and took a sip of his beer.

"I'm Dez, and this is Hannah." Hannah gave a small wave and smiled. "Did you catch the guys on the Elevation Tour a few years back?"

Professor Ulrich nodded. "I saw all four shows that week in Boston. It was one of the greatest experiences of my life."

Dez's face lit up as he finished the remainder of his drink. "That is absolutely incredible...I was at all four too." He patted the professor on his right shoulder and smiled.

Professor Ulrich winked at Dez and reached for his beer on the bar. "They're one of my favorite bands. I teach at Northern Boston University, and usually once very few semesters I try to slip in a class directed around Bono's lyrics."

"That is really awesome, Professor." Dez shook his beer bottle, realizing it was nearly empty. He smiled at Hannah and asked her what she wanted to drink. He then looked at the professor. "How 'bout you? What're you drinking?"

"I'll take another beer," Professor Ulrich replied.

Outside, more people were filing into Vincenzo's. The bouncer at the front door graciously greeted the club's guests, checking IDs and waving patrons inside.

It was nearing the midnight hour.

CHAPTER 17

▼

Faith adjusted the blue studded belt around her waist and ate the olive in her martini glass. Looking at the clock, she could see it was already well past midnight. "Where the hell is he?" she asked herself, scanning the length of the bar for her ex-husband.

Looking at the opposite side of the bar, she could see him laughing and talking to a group of guys that looked significantly younger than him. Faith groaned and began to walk over to Professor Ulrich.

"For me, The Clash were a far more influential band than The Dead Boys ever were," she could overhear him saying.

"I'll have to disagree with you," a guy with tight pants replied to her ex-husband. "It's all about style and stage presence, which the Boys just had so much more of."

"You've got a point. Hey Faith, come meet these guys." The professor motioned to Dez, Johnny and Chester, who all gave some sort of nonchalant wave to her. "This is Dez, Johnny and Chester. I came over here to get a drink and we all just chatting about some old school rock music."

Faith felt a slight twinge of happiness for him. "Oh, that's cool. However, Bruce, you *should* be acting your age." She giggled and rubbed his arm.

"Hey, these guys really know their shit." The professor nodded in the group's direction. "You need another drink, Faith?"

Faith shook her head. "No thanks, I'm all set. I'm just itching to head over to Ryan's Diner." She flipped back her blonde bangs and took her seat at a barstool.

"You guys are going to Ryan's Diner, too?" Dez perked up and got up out of his seat. "We were planning on heading over there as soon as we left the bar." He looked over at Hannah. "Would you like to join us?"

Hannah closed one eye and brought her lips closer together. "I'd love to, but I've got a really long ride out back home. I'm practically on the other side of Massachusetts." She frowned and gave Dez a kiss on the cheek.

Dez felt a wayward realm of strangeness consume his body. He stood in shock until the words on the tip of his tongue were able to be released. He hadn't felt the softly damp touch of a woman's kiss since the last time he saw Koral. "I'm sorry. It's okay, though."

"Listen, babe, here's my number." Hannah reached for a pen out of her purse and scrawled digits on the corner of a napkin. She folded it in half and handed to Dez, who was trying to contain his joy. "Give me a call sometime."

Dez shoved the folded cocktail napkin into his front pocket and took a sip of his beer, masking how good he felt to have actually generated interest from another female. Looking at Hannah, he didn't see her age. All Dez could see was the sparkling pulchritude in her eyes. "Thanks," he humbly said to her.

"I haven't seen my friends in a while; they're probably wondering where the hell I disappeared off to." Hannah packed up her purse and finished the remaining drops of her drink. Leaning over to adjust the lace on one of her boots, Dez could not help himself but to look at her large pale breasts as they hung underneath her blouse. "Sweetie, I'm going to gather my friends and head out of here. It was nice meeting all of you." She smiled at the group before pulling Dez off to the side.

"Hey honey, I hope you're not freaked out by how old I am." Her eyes presented a heavy sense of sincerity. "If the age difference bothers you, I completely understand."

Dez took a deep breath and hid his urge to grin. "Hannah, don't worry about it. I'll give you a call during the week." The words felt oddly right for him to say as he leaned in to give her a kiss on the cheek.

Hannah's pale cheeks began to turn red as she walked away from Dez. Taking steps back to her group of friends, Dez watched as her tight body swayed in the low light of the club. He put his head down and experienced a moment of happiness. He walked over to rejoin his friends, both old and new.

"If you like women that old, I have a few friends I could introduce you to," Faith proclaimed with a laugh to Dez upon his return to the group. The professor nudged his ex-wife and gave her a look of disappointment. Dez winked at her and sat on an open barstool. "We should all head over to Ryan's together when we leave," Faith added while jokingly punching Dez on the arm.

"Sounds good to me," said the professor.

Chester, who for most the night had been nearly completely silent, jerked his hand up and slapped Dez on the back. "What did I tell ya, buddy? You're too good-looking not to be able to pick up women at a bar."

Professor Ulrich threw his arm around Dez and tried to mess up his hair. "Good job, man. Your friends have been telling me that you've been having a rough summer."

"Well, it has been tough so far," Dez replied. "But I'm sure I'll pick myself up out of the rut and wind up being okay." He smiled and looked at the clock hanging over a picture of Frank Sinatra on the bar's wall. "You guys want to leave soon? Ryan's is probably going to be packed. Professor, are you and Faith coming along?"

Faith nodded as the professor looked at Dez. "We used to go there back when we were married, but neither of us has been there in a while. Suffice to say that we're both interested in their pancakes," Professor Ulrich said with a hearty laugh.

Faith walked over to the women's bathroom as Chester and Johnny went to check out an old-school style jukebox in the corner of the club, which neither of them had noticed until recently.

"I'm really glad I ran into you and your friends," the professor said to Dez. "Even though you don't know a lot about me, it's been tough being here tonight with Faith."

Dez presented a look of confusion and tilted his head. "You know, I might have just caught this, but…you and Faith are divorced, aren't you?"

Professor Ulrich nodded in agreement. "Yup." He contemplated informing Dez of the Venus transit. It didn't take long to realize that his new friend seemed like a genuine person. "Dez, this might sound completely fucking crazy, but hear me out for a minute."

"Sure thing, Professor. What's on your mind?" Dez fixed his rolled up sleeves and waited for the professor to talk. For the first time of the evening, he felt a minor buzz from the evening's multiple beers.

"You know what, forget about it. I'm sorry." The professor relinquished all of the fear he had been feeling regarding the transit. He buried deep within his mind and tried to change the subject, even though it was him who had nearly brought about the impending tragedy of the evening. "I need to take a piss. I'll be right back."

Professor Ulrich stood up and began walking to the bathroom. Passing by crowds of women dancing, his mind focused on the unassisted ignorance of humanity. He and a few others were the only ones who had the slightest idea of what the Venus transit could possibility bring. Faith, Dez, everyone else…he felt the need to protect them.

Walking past a man in a purple leisure suit, he couldn't help but let his mind drift out of a serious notion. He giggled to himself and walked into the bathroom. Stepping over to a sink near the wall, he turned on the water and scooped a generous amount of cold liquid into his hands. Splashing his face, he let the coolness calm his nerves.

The undertone of terror began to grip his body once again as he caught a glimpse of the moon outside of the bathroom window. Looking at his watch, it was 12:41. The transit would be beginning in nearly half an hour.

The professor gathered his thoughts and scratched his head. As the whole day had dictated, confusion had reigned supreme. Shrugging it off, he realized all he wanted to do was protect Faith. Even though the past year forced him into a realm of loss and pain, the likes of which he had never before experienced, he still loved her.

Professor Ulrich spit into the sink and turned off the water. Reaching into his pocket, he pulled out his cell phone. There was no cell service inside of the building.

He felt the need to concoct a plan for the rest of the night. He was glad that he had met Dez and his crew, as being with a large group might be better off if anything should happen to occur. The professor could see how Faith thought he was crazy; anyone would have thought the same.

Professor Ulrich was stuck in limbo. There was nothing he could do until the transit had actually begun to take shape.

Walking out of the bathroom, the entire club seemed to be moving in slow motion. A woman dressed completely in white swayed back and forth as if time were nowhere to be found. The DJ was waving his right fist in the air, sending the crowded dance floor into frenzy.

Professor Ulrich saw Faith sitting at the bar, conversing with Dez. *I'm definitely still in love with her,* his mind had told him. *Look at her, she's absolutely stunning.*

With a bellowing sigh, the professor walked up behind her.

"Professor, we're going to finish these drinks up and then head out." Dez pointed to the last few sips contained in his bottle. "Cool with you?"

The professor nodded and looked at his watch. He closed his eyes and blew air out of his mouth.

"Are you alright?" asked Dez, who had a look of concern upon his face.

"I'm fine," replied the professor. "I'm just fine."

CHAPTER 18

▼

Dez reached into his front pockets to check for any remaining dollar bills. He found a few that were crumpled up and slipped them to the bartender, who was gathering the mass of empty bottles and glasses that the group had created.

For the first time in a couple of months, he had felt better about life. Nights out with friends after the Koral breakup had never helped to alleviate the dampened mood he had found himself stuck in. Tonight was an unusually uncharacteristic evening for Dez and his friends.

He was enjoying the company of Professor Ulrich and Faith, and was excited about having the group come together at Ryan's Diner for some late-night food. Looking over Chester and Johnny, who both seemed somewhat jovial, Dez pulled out his cell phone to call Nathan.

While scrolling for his brother's number, he saw that he had no service signal. "Fuck," he said aloud.

Faith was engaged in conversation with Chester. "You're still young. By the time you've spent over 10 years in the mental health field, I can almost guarantee that you'll get sick of it, Chester."

"I'm enjoying it so far," he replied. "The place that I'm at right now is working out well for me. I'm hoping to continue working there while I'm getting my Master's degree." Chester's meth high had worn off, but he wasn't interested in doing anymore for the evening.

"Give it time, honey, give it time." Faith nodded her head and looked over at her ex-husband, who was staring at the clock on the bar wall. "Bruce, you're really not worried about that transit thing, are you?"

Professor Ulrich turned to her with a look of disbelief. "Please, Faith, not in front of anyone." He grabbed Faith's arm tightly and quickly let go.

Faith apologized and changed the subject of conversation. "Well, boys, are we almost ready to head out of here?"

Johnny chugged almost an entire bottle of beer and burped loudly. "Yeah, I'd say we're about done here." His brown spiked hair had started to curl because of the heat within Vincenzo's.

"What happened to that older chick you were talking to?" Chester asked his friend. "Did she find out you were 30 years younger than her?" He chuckled and playfully shoved Johnny.

"No, you asshole." Johnny's stern look gave off his feelings of discontent with the evening. "She ended up having three kids and a husband. I think she just wanted to flirt with me for the sake of proving that she was still attractive."

"That sucks, bro." Dez frowned and checked his cell phone again. There was still no signal. "Okay, let's call it a night."

The group made their way to the club's entrance. Professor Ulrich checked his watch and shook his hand about. A few seconds later, he glanced at his watch again. It was a few minutes past 1 a.m.

Dez noticed the professor doing this, and pulled him aside. "Professor, are you sure everything's alright?"

Professor Ulrich looked directly into Dez's eyes. "Honestly, Dez, no, everything is not alright." The professor had made a quick decision and struggled to find the words describe what he thought might me a tragic night for all. "Listen to me carefully. Something horrible is going to happen tonight."

Dez backed away from the professor and flinched a puzzled look. "What's the problem?"

Taking a deep breath, the professor collected his thoughts. "You've seen the coverage of the Venus transit, correct? It's been all over the newspapers and television."

"Yeah, I thought it looked kind of interesting." Before Dez could speak any more words, the professor had gripped his shoulders with both hands.

"My assistant and I found a document that dates back to the last time this transit occurred in 1882. It was a letter written by a little girl." Professor Ulrich paused and looked away. "The letter said that when the transit took place, it caused absolute destruction in Revmont. I know, it sounds really fucking insane. Why am I the only one to know about this? Is this a joke? Is this for real? Dez, I've been struggling with these questions all frigging week."

Dez's pupils had increased in size. Words could not been formed in his mind. His lips remained closed tightly.

"Dez, you have to believe me. I can't go to the police. I can't tell any officials. Who is actually going to believe me?" The professor's attitude urged his feelings of abandon. "For all I know, this transit could roll around and nothing will happen. A bunch of science junkies like me will watch something that hasn't been seen in 112 years. But, I will *not* discount the possibility of absolute horror bracing us all tonight."

Dez found himself with a look of shock embracing his face. "Professor, I really don't know what to say. I am a firm believer of strange things happening in this world, but that sounds *really* fucked up." The rest of the group was already outside.

Dez continued on. "So, is this supposed to happen all around the world? Just the East Coast? Just Revmont? Tell me, Professor."

Professor Ulrich's hands shook. "I don't know what to tell you, Dez. I haven't had adequate time to research this. I'm uncertain if there's something in Revmont that will react to the alignment of the planets tonight."

"What are we supposed to do? Hang around Foree Cemetary and see if the dead break through their coffins and attack us?" Dez could feel his natural attitude coming out as the words flew out of his mouth. "What the fuck are we going to do? You know if you tell the rest of the group they're just going to laugh at you."

"Faith knows. But she's not a very receptive person, Dez." Professor Ulrich had finally let go of his tight grip on Dez's shoulders. "We have to play this cool; just let the night go as planned and let's see what happens. It seems fucked up to stand here and say something like that, but we have no other option."

Dez sighed and shook his head. "I guess you're right. We can't do anything else. I can't even believe I'm standing here *myself* if this shit is really going to go down."

"Listen, just go on with the night, Dez. We can't take any action because we don't know if anything is happening for sure." The professor felt helpless. The truth was that there really was nothing he could do.

Dez grabbed the professor's arm and motioned to join up with the rest of the group, who were probably wondering where the two had gone. Upon pushing the entrance doors open to the outside, Dez suddenly felt what was once a pleasant evening turn into something he could not describe.

Pulling out his cell phone, he dialed Nathan's number and brought the object to his ear. "Hey little bro, we're leaving the club now. Can you meet us at Ryan's in about a half hour? Forty-five minutes? Sounds good, Nathan." He flipped the cell phone to its normal position and dropped it back into his jacket pocket.

"Yeah, she did kind of look like Dolly Parton, didn't she?" Chester was describing a woman he had danced with inside earlier. "She had these huge boobs." Faith leaned over to him and pinched his ear.

"Is Nathan meeting us at the diner?" Johnny asked Dez.

"Yeah, he's just getting out of a movie with his girlfriend. He's going to drop her off and swing by Ryan's," replied Dez. He looked over at the professor. "You guys know how to get there, right?"

"I haven't been there in about a year, but I'm sure I still know the way," Faith said. "We'll follow you anyways, though, just in case we get lost." She turned to Professor Ulrich, who was staring up into the sky. "Bruce, I'll drive. Okay?"

"That's fine." Professor Ulrich tried hard to look into the sky, wondering how close Venus was to the start of the transit. He looked at his watch. It was 1:11. According to most published reports, the transit would be beginning in two minutes.

CHAPTER 19

▼

Chester tossed his car keys to Dez, who caught them and gave his friend a baffled look. "It looked like you were okay to drive, bro. The past hour or so you've been out of your "high." Dez leaned against Chester's car. Johnny was already inside, sitting in the backseat.

"I don't feel very good, Dez. Just do me a favor and drive." Chester clutched his stomach and tilted his head back. "I'll be fine, it's just my stomach. I haven't eaten all day and that last hit was a little too much for me."

Dez patted him on the back. "Just let know if we need to pull over, dude." He opened the passenger side door for Chester and looped around the front end of the car. Opening the driver's side door, he plopped down into the seat and looked into the rear view mirror to check out his hair. "So, what do you guys think of the professor and his ex-wife?"

Johnny erupted from the backseat. "That's his ex-wife? Shit, it looked as if they were still together." He leaned over Chester to look inside the glove compartment. "Fuck, there's no gum in here. Professor Ulrich was pretty cool. He really seems to know his music shit. And Faith was just hot." Johnny laughed and looked over at Dez.

Chester removed his hands from his belly and rolled down the window. "That professor guy was pretty cool. Faith and I were talking a lot about working in the medical field. And you, Mister Dez, you scored a number tonight. I'm very, very proud of you."

Dez giggled as he turned on the car's engine. "Well, she's a little old for me. But I think she's attractive, not to mention extremely charming." He smiled while pulling out of the parking spot.

Flashing his high beams to Faith, who was driving in front of him, he drove around her to the front of the parking lot's exit. Turning on the radio, he flipped the dial to one of Boston's bigger rock radio stations to hear Metallica's "Sad But True."

"Well, Dez, if anything, it just proved that you *are* able to pick up women. Fuck all of that Koral bullshit, it's done with," Johnny said from the backseat while playing air drums to the song. "Besides, it's been a couple months now, you should be working your way to feeling better about it all."

Dez wished he could agree with his friend. Even though landing Hannah's number had boosted his confidence and self-esteem, his heart was still blackened and cold from the pain Koral had caused him.

After a few minutes, Dez was driving on the highway. With the windows down, the cool night air began to fill the car.

*   *   *   *

The moon was shining upon the tombstones of Foree Cemetery, sending a calm projection of light across the rows of the dead. The branches of the trees were swaying slightly within the cool Revmont breeze.

Flashes of headlights would sometimes bounce off the stones as cars would pass by. A raccoon bounced lightly about a row of gravestones.

In the sky, Venus was beginning to make its stunning display in the realm of space. The alignment was beginning; the celestial phenomenon could not be stopped. Shifting into the crosshairs of the sun's orbit, the dark planet edged its way into a starry coalition with the earth.

Down below and back on Earth, the grass of Foree Cemetery began to shake lightly. It was the not the breeze, however, that was sending it into a slight motion. Rustles from underneath the ground could be heard as the tombstones began to reverberate.

The raccoon perked up its small ears as it ran across a particular gravesite. With the night sky beaming down into the graveyard, the bodies underneath began to moan with horrific delight. Pushing their way through the softened wood of their post-worldly containers, the supple dirt gave way to their disgustingly fleshy claws, eager to make their way through to the world above their own.

The sordid hands finally broke free of their underground chambers, throwing away small mounds of dirt as they pushed their way to the moonlight. The moans were growing louder as more and more of the dead had broken free of their ghastly prisons.

*   *   *   *

Professor Ulrich leaned his head against the passenger window and stared at the night world outside of Faith's car.

Thoughts of uncertainty plagued his mind. What was he doing sitting next to Faith? The professor thought of all the nights that he sat alone in his living room, wondering how the one woman who changed his life had divorced him because she simply had too many personal issues to deal with.

"You can change the radio station if you want, Bruce." Faith peered over at her ex-husband and smiled. "I know you keep up with all of these new bands coming out. I can't stand most of them."

Professor Ulrich laughed and began searching through the radio stations on the dial. "Vincenzo's had a good amount of decent music tonight. Is it always like that?"

Faith nodded and flipped her directional to take the Revmont exit off the interstate highway. "It depends on the night. We lucked out tonight with the music."

The professor only remembered some of Revmont's landmarks when Faith turned into the city. Going to Ryan's Diner would certainly be an experience for him this evening; being in the restaurant would surely bring about memories of better days.

Faith continued along one of Revmont's near-empty streets. Out of the corner of his eye, Professor Ulrich saw a large, cathedral-style church in which he could remember passing by years ago. The ominous backdrop of the church's bell tower creepily created a sinister match with the onslaught of the night sky.

"Is Ryan's off of Belmont Ave.? Or do I have to keep going a little further?" Faith tossed back her long blonde bangs and turned to the professor, who was watching the sight of the church pass out of his line of vision.

"I'm not sure. I haven't been here in forever, Faith." He shook his head and rolled up his window halfway. It was getting colder outside.

"Oh, there it is!" Faith shouted and her voice squeaked. Professor Ulrich tried to contain his glorious laugh, but failed. "Very funny, Bruce. I know I still sometimes sound like I'm 15 years old."

Pulling into the parking lot of Ryan's Diner, the professor noticed his new group of friends had just pulled in themselves. Dez was leaning against the car while talking on his cell phone.

Faith aligned her car right next to Chester's. Both she and the professor opened their doors and got out of the car.

"That is a sweet fucking ride!" Johnny pointed at Faith's car and then gave her a high five.

"Sounds like a plan, Nathan. I'll see you in a few." Dez flipped his cell phone closed and turned the rest of the group. "My little bro should be here in about 15 minutes. Let's just get a table and he'll meet us inside when he gets here."

The group walked ahead of Professor Ulrich, who pulled Dez back. "Dez, I'm sorry if I sounded completely crazy earlier." He looked at his watch and realized that it was almost 2 a.m., nearly 45 full minutes into the Venus transit. "I think my imagination and realm of paranormal science has really gotten the best of my better judgment."

Dez smiled and playfully shoved the professor. "It's cool, Professor. I can kind of understand that neither of us are in the best frames of mind nowadays. Come on, I'm starving. Hopefully there won't be too long of a wait."

"Is this place still home to those drunken night owls that have just poured out of all the Boston bars?" Professor Ulrich stood on the tips of his toes and tried to look inside the diner. "Looks like it is," he said with a laugh, noticing the swaying post-teenagers trying to keep their balance in the lobby.

Dez pulled open the door to the restaurant and motioned for the professor to walk in. Coming through the second set of doors, Dez could smell the quality of greasy diner food, one that brought him back to the last time he had been to Ryan's Diner. Thinking back, it was with Koral, he had realized.

Dez momentarily lapsed into memories with Koral. It had been the middle of October; Koral was visiting for the weekend and the two had just spent a full day in Salem. She was filled with joy all day at the fact of being in the same city where the infamous Salem Witch Trials had occurred.

The scent of Halloween had always had a firm grip on Dez. Having the love of his life next to him and walking hand-in-hand in the nation's Halloween capital had elicited the highest of times for him. The two had made a late-night trip to Ryan's Diner for food after going to see a movie.

Koral was wearing a black skirt with blue stars garnering the sides. Her fishnet tights and tall black boots sent Dez into frenzy, he could remember. He recalled sitting on the same side of a booth in the diner, draping a hand across his girlfriend's thigh while waiting for an order of pancakes to arrive. Koral had complained all day of how much it hurt to walk in those boots.

Dez shook the pain from his body and opened his eyes. Johnny was looking clearly exhausted. Chester was leaning against the wall. Professor Ulrich and

Faith were chatting quietly on the bench next to the hostess' podium. Dez walked over to the chunky hostess.

"Table for six, please. Booth in the back if you can." Dez winked at her and turned back to his group.

Professor Ulrich jumped out of his seat as Faith attempted to lay her head on his shoulder. He calmed down quickly and let it happen.

"Bruce, do you remember when we used to stroll in here wasted out of our minds?" She was playing with the sleeves of her sweatshirt.

Professor Ulrich thought back to the days when they were still married. Even thought it was somewhat out of the way, he always gave in to Faith's requests to eat at Ryan's whenever they were drinking in Boston.

He looked down at Faith, who was still playing with the bottom of her sleeves. She still looked beautiful. Her flawless body, her shapely breasts, her uncanny smile…it all made the professor want to forget all of the games she had played over the past year. A part of his mind wanted to ask her to reconsider the divorce.

"You guys are all set. Follow me." The hostess grabbed six menus from the inside of the podium and started to walk into the back section of the restaurant. Dez looked over the cliché groups of drunken twenty-somethings as they laughed and attempted to shovel greasy mounds of breakfast foods into their mouths.

Ryan's Diner was a staple for late-night dining in Revmont; it was packed almost every weekend with crowds of both younger people and adults alike. Dez could remember some of his earliest memories of the place as he took his seat on the end of the booth cushion. The smell of syrup stained the inside of his nostrils.

The rest of the group filed into both sides of the booth. Faith's touch to the professor sent a slight shiver throughout his body as she leaned against his side. "Are you comfortable, honey?" she asked him.

Professor Ulrich nodded and reached for his cell phone in attempt to kill the moment. He saw that he had a voicemail from Dane. Bringing the phone to his ear, he dialed his voicemail.

"Hey Professor," the voicemail said. "It's almost 2 a.m. and it looks like nothing has happened. I'm sitting in the middle of Revmont Town Square. Maybe we just became overworked for no reason at all. I feel like a fool, but I'm glad I'm not the only one." Dane laughed. "Well, I'm going to lean back here in this comfy seat and get some much-needed reading done."

Professor Ulrich clicked the phone shut and tossed it back into his suit jacket pocket. He looked at his watch. Dane was right; feeling like a fool was the only way to sense right now. He could overhear a radio broadcast that a cook about 10 feet away was listening to.

We're here live in the heart of Boston at the Commons. There's about a hundred people huddled in the cool June air, patiently awaiting for the early morning sun to rise so they can be witness to a cosmic miracle. We'll be broadcasting all night and giving some of these patrons an opportunity to share their excitement. Keep your dial tuned right here. We've got another five in a row coming up, starting with some Pearl Jam.

The professor's attention shifted as the waitress approached the group's table. She was older, possibly in her late 50s. Her dark brown hair was tied up in a bun, and her apron was stained with various types of food residue. "Can I start you all of with some drinks," she asked the table.

Dez cleared his throat and smiled at the waitress. "I'll have some orange juice."

CHAPTER 20

▼

Nathan tapped his hands on the steering wheel as he pulled into the diner's parking lot. He immediately saw Chester's car and attempted to find a spot close to it.

Shutting off the car engine, he reached for his Boston Red Sox cap out of the backseat and adjusted it on his head. He searched the passenger side for his cell phone, but couldn't find it. "Shit, I must have left it at Lauren's house," he said to himself.

Walking over to Ryan's Diner, he could see the restaurant was packed, as he had expected it to be. Pulling open the first set of glass doors, Nathan could barely make out his older brother's hair from afar.

He smiled to the waitress after walking through the second set of doors and headed for the rear of the diner. After passing a group of people whom he thought he may have went to high school with, he had approached Dez and the others.

"Dez dude, so it looked like you totally hit it off with that mid-life crisis gothic woman," Johnny said with a hearty laugh. Dez frowned and tossed a sugar packet at his friend.

"So, what's this I hear about a gothic chick, bro?" Nathan grinned and sat down at the only open spot at the booth. "How's it going, guys?"

Dez leaned forward in his seat. "Nathan, this is Faith and Professor Ulrich. We met them at the club we went to tonight. They used to always come here." Dez nodded at the couple.

Professor Ulrich reached his hand over to Nathan. "Nice to meet you, Nathan. Your brother tells me you've been looking into colleges. If you're thinking about Northern Boston University, I could pull some strings."

Nathan cleared his throat. "That's awesome. I'm planning on taking some time off before I head back to school. I'm enjoying some of the freedom right now."

"Sure thing. Just let your brother know when you want me to give you a tour of the school." The professor smiled and took a sip of his Diet Coke. "We held off on ordering food until you got here."

Nathan nodded and turned to Chester, who was pouring packets of sugar into his large glass of iced tea. "You look like you had fun tonight." Nathan punched him in the arm and turned his head to motion for the waitress.

Chester groaned and shot Nathan a dirty look. "Ask your brother about his little woman."

"Come on guys, she was way too old for me," Dez said, warranting a pinch from Faith. "Well, Faith, I would say you look like you're not even five or six years older than me. Hannah was beautiful, but I don't think a relationship with that kind of age difference would even work out."

The professor winked at Dez. "Just give her a call anyways, Dez. It can't hurt." He took another sip of his drink and then used his straw to stir the ice at the bottom. The feelings of terror in his uncertainty had started to fade away. He watched his reflection in the window across from the booth. Professor Ulrich perceived himself to be strung out and exhausted; he could notice the uneasiness in the way his reflection moved.

The waitress made her way over to the table. "Ok gang, are we all ready to order?"

Chester ordered a small stack of pancakes, Johnny asked for a plate of French fries, as well as another glass of apple juice. "We're going to split a tall stack of buttermilk pancakes," Professor Ulrich said to the waitress. "Dez, you're next."

Dez thumbed his way down the plastic menu. "Hmmm...I'll just have an order of toast and a short stack." Nathan informed the waitress that he wanted the same thing. An old man sitting in the booth next to the group was reading the day's *Boston Globe*. The headline read: *Rare Venus transit to occur this evening.*

Professor Ulrich caught the same sight and sighed. Faith was pulling him closer to her, but he tried to edge his body away.

"Tonight has been such a boring night," Nathan said as he leaned back in the booth.

With a loud crash, the window near the booth next to the group's shattered in hundreds of pieces. A large figure had burst through the opening. Its ragged and bloody hands had enveloped the old man's throat, squeezing his neck as the gross creature tore a large piece of flesh from his face. The screams from the old man pierced the air.

In matter of seconds, the figure had dug its hands deep into the elderly man's chest, ripping out chunks of his internal organs as blood has spurted all over the table and onto the floor.

"What the fuck!" screamed Dez from across the way. Before he could say anything else, the entire diner was encompassed in a panic as hoards of the staff and patrons alike rushed for the entrance.

Professor Ulrich grabbed Faith's arm and motioned for the group to get away from the area. "Everyone! The fire exit!" Faith shoved the door open and the rest of the group followed. Chester and Johnny rushed through the opening, as the professor held the door open for Dez and Nathan.

Looking behind him, Professor Ulrich gasped in awe as he saw other zombie-like creatures bursting through the other windows of the diner. The table's waitress was caught in the grip of one of the monsters as it tore her right cheek off and devoured it with horrific intention.

"Bruce, get out of there!" Faith screamed from outside. It was happening. It was really happening. The professor stood in shock until Dez grabbed his arm and dragged him outside of the fire exit.

Slamming the door shut behind them, Dez hunched over to catch his breath. "It's fucking happening, Professor!" Faith started to cry and hung onto her ex-husband's arm.

"What exactly is going on here?" Chester shouted at the top of his lungs. "We have to get the hell out of here, right now!" The groans of other creatures were heard as the group looked over to the parking lot. Four of the undead were lurching towards them, arms out raised, hungry for blood and destruction.

"Let's just get the hell out of here. Everyone's got to get into Chester's car, right now!" Nathan was the first to jump towards the vehicle. With a quick right jab, he socked the closest figure to him, sending it to the ground. Faith and Professor Ulrich quickly ran towards the car, followed by Dez, who narrowly escaped the lunge of a creature who grabbed and ripped part of his black shirt.

Chester tossed his keys to Johnny, who was already at the car. As he tried to unlock the driver's side door, a creature behind the bushes tackled him and sunk its rotting yellow teeth into his arm. Johnny yelped in pain as the keys fell out of his reach.

"Johnny! Oh my God!" Faith leaned down to help Johnny, who was bracing his right arm. Loads of blood oozed from the deep cut of the wound. The dark figure lurched again, this time at Faith. The professor lunged in front of the creature, knocking it abound.

"Faith, grab the goddamn keys," Professor Ulrich said to ex-wife, pointing the set of keys on the pavement. Faith left Johnny's side and reached for the keys.

Dez took action and grabbed his brother. "Nathan, your car is on the other side. I don't see any of them over here. I'm going to help them out; drive your car back over here. We have to get the fuck out of here. Hurry up!" Nathan nodded and ran to his car.

Dez gathered Professor Ulrich and Faith, who were on the ground next to Johnny. The other creatures were attacking who was left inside of the diner. "Nathan's bringing his car around. We don't know how long before more of those things have filled this area. We have to find somewhere safe to hide out."

"He's right. We have to get out of here and into someplace safe." Professor Ulrich's hands were shaking. "I can't believe it really happened. Jesus!" He screamed and started to lose his self-control.

"Bruce, Bruce...there was nothing you could do." Faith's sparkling blue eyes presented a short sense of calm over the terrifying situation at hand. "None of us believed you. But we can't think about that now. We just have to get out of here, Bruce."

Chester could hear the loud engine of Nathan's car. "There's Nathan. Quick, Professor, help me pick up Johnny." The professor nodded and leaned down to pick up the wounded Johnny, was still clutching his arm. The blood had stained most of his clothes.

Faith was the first to grab onto the door handle of Nathan's car. Swinging the door open, she motioned to Professor Ulrich, who was holding up Johnny. The cut looked severe and unwarranted, Faith thought to herself.

With droplets of blood spilling across the professor's arm, he attempted to ease Johnny into the car. Out of the corner his eye, he could see more of the undead slowly stumbling out of nearby areas, attacking the panicked crowds that were filling the streets. "Chester, lift up his legs," he shouted to Chester.

Chester hesitated before helping his friend into the vehicle. A feeling of shock encompassed his body as he looked past the frightened group and into the diner, past the shards of broken window. All he could make out was smears of dark red.

Dez, who was standing a few feet away, was trying to watch for attackers as the group piled into his brother's car. One of the scrappy beings blindsided him in an attempt to feast on his arm. Its gigantic and near-shattered teeth were poised to rip into Dez's arm, but he shoved off the creature to the ground with the other arm and held its throat with the heel of his thick black boot.

"Fucker," Dez spat out after giving the undead monster a kick to the temple, sending spools of blood into the night air. He looked down upon his attacker. Its eyes were jet black, staring into the evil space surrounding the evening sky. The tattered rags covering the being were torn, revealing decaying masses of flesh. The smell of death quickly wavered its way into Dez's nostrils.

Nathan beeped the horn at Dez. He stuck his head out the window. "Dez, get in the car before another one of those things grabs a hold of you!" Nathan motioned with his left hand towards his brother.

Dez jogged to the car and opened the front door, where Faith was sitting with a concerned look upon her face. Her blonde hair was tossed about and beads of sweat had began to form around her eyebrows.

Squeezing in next to her, Dez quickly closed the car door and looked at Nathan, who had a blank expression on his face. "Well, what the fuck do we do now?" asked Dez as he shot a glance over at the professor, who was holding onto Johnny. Looking down at his wound, Dez could see scrapes of darkened blood oozing out of the deepened cut.

"There's got to be somewhere that's out of the public eye where we can hide out until morning. If my thoughts are correct, the transit only lasts a little over six hours." Professor Ulrich tried his hardest to not allow his paranoia to affect his suggestion. "We can only hope that the end of the transit means the end of those undead creatures. Their power is a direct and cohesive parallel with the transit, I believe."

With a loud bang, a putrefied fist shattered the back window of Nathan's car, sending shards of glass across the inside of the vehicle. "Move, Nathan!" Chester shouted from the backseat.

Nathan stepped on the gas pedal and sped towards the exit of Ryan's Diner's parking lot. As he was about to turn right onto the main street, he caught a glimpse of what looked like a child standing in the middle of the road.

Nathan slowed down the vehicle as the vision appeared clearer. The child was dressed in a 19th century-styled suit, with ruffles of white fabric around the opening the outfit's sleeves. The boy's blonde hair revealed a strong stitching around his hairline, most likely the cause of his death years ago.

"Just do it, bro. He's fucking dead! Just run him over!" Dez screamed at his brother, whose eyes were watering from the sick situation ahead of him. Faith continued crying next to the two brothers in the front seat. She reached her hand over to Dez, who squeezed it tightly.

Nathan took a deep breath and paused. His mind flashed back to a child playing with his mother's groceries at Nathan's store. He thought of the giant smile on the boy's face as he flung a can of string beans to the ground, warranting a laugh from an elderly woman in the aisle.

"Nathan, we need to get the hell out of here." Professor Ulrich gripped the driver's shoulder and nodded. Nathan put his head down and stared at the center of the car's steering wheel.

In what seemed like slow motion, Nathan pushed down on the gas pedal, sending the speedometer dial into frenzy as the car careened forward on the road. The child gurgled a noise through his mouth as the front end of Nathan's car bashed into his upper torso, forcing the boy's right arm to detach from his body. The rest of the child was caught under the back wheels of the car, producing a sickening thud.

Faith moaned as she looked into the right side mirror. The undead child's body was crumpled in the middle of the empty street, looking desolate and lonely in the mess of the night.

She wrung onto Dez's hand, digging her lengthy nails into his soft skin.

"St. Knight's Church!" shouted Dez, to the surprise of the rest of the passengers. "Nathan, get there right the fuck right now." Nathan shot back a puzzled look while trying to keep a close eye on the road in front of him.

"Professor, we need to find someplace to hide, right?" Dez looked to the backseat. "St. Knight's closed down a little over two months ago. If we can break in, I'm sure we'll stand a better chance of living until the morning when the transit is over."

Faith looked up at Dez. "What about Johnny? We need to get him cleaned up before that cut gets any worse."

"If there's a first aid kit at the church, we'll be able to buy some time and take him to a hospital in the morning," Chester said from the backseat. He wiped the sweat from his brow. "From the looks of it, the hospital is going to be pretty busy in the morning."

"St. Knight's Church it is." Nathan sped faster on the street. The group looked in horror as other areas of Revmont were in complete and utter chaos. Dez stared at beaten-up white pickup truck that was turned over on its side. Three members of the undead army were grabbing at the driver, who was stuck inside the small inside of the vehicle.

Dez could hear his loud screams echo through the air as one of the creatures ripped apart his stomach, revealing the gooey insides of the man's organs. The other two kneeled down as they brought huge chunks of innards to their mouths, allowing the blood to smear all over their decomposed faces.

"Jesus," whispered Faith as her eyes fixated on the scene on the side of the road. She wiped the salty discharge from her eyes and leaned her head on Dez's shoulder.

The high bell tower of St. Knight's Church appeared in the night sky. Dez glanced at the ominous look of the dark brick that made up the building as Nathan turned into the empty parking lot. What once was a normal sight for Dez in Revmont soon became the sight of hope and survival.

CHAPTER 21

▼

Professor Ulrich took one of Nathan's work uniform shirts from the floor of the car and wrapped it tightly around Johnny's arm. The blood had started to congeal around his arm, presenting a sinister mess.

Nathan shut off the car's engine and looked over at the group. "What are we going to do if we can't get the door open?" he asked.

Dez had already gotten out of the car and motioned for his brother to pop open the trunk. He surveyed the parking lot for anyone hiding in the shadows before hearing the clunk of the trunk's hood open slightly.

Looking into the trunk, Dez shoved aside a copy of last month's *Maxim,* a container of tennis balls and a thick, navy blue gas station attendant's jacket until he found what he was looking for: a jet black wooden baseball bat that the brothers had used during pickup games with locals from in and around Revmont.

"This will have to do," he whispered to himself while taking a practice swing. Dez closed the trunk and opened the right backseat door. "I don't see any of those things around. Let's make a quick entrance into the church while we can."

Professor Ulrich got out of the car first, still clutching Johnny, who had turned pale, red circle around his eyes. Chester held a firm grip around his friend's back and attempted to ease him to his feet.

Faith stepped out of the vehicle and ran to the professor, who welcomed her with a kiss on the forehead. "Faith, I swear I won't let anything happen to you," he said while gripping her with his free arm. "Don't cry, we're going to be okay."

The stairs of St. Knight's Church loomed ahead. Dez gripped the bat close to his chest as he allowed the rest of the group to travel in front of him. The professor and Chester helped Johnny up the stairs while Faith followed close behind. As

Dez put his foot on the first step of the church's entrance, he heard a scraping sound behind him.

With a quick motion, the creature draped his arm around Dez, bringing him to the ground as it lost its balance and fell back. Faith screamed and the others turned around to see their friend battle on the pavement near the stairs.

Its rotting teeth poised in a mix of saliva and blood, the creature fought for a chunk of Dez's flesh. Professor Ulrich let go of Johnny and let Chester bear the weight of the wounded man as he hopped the down the entire flight of church stairs.

Dez was now on the bottom of the wrestle, with the undead monster's hands gripping his throat while trying to catch a piece of the former in its mouth. The professor launched an elbow into it, allowing Dez to break free and slide towards the bat, which was thrown a few feet away from him.

Dez picked up the object and arched his back, looking for a good shot. He stepped back and took a swing, catching the creature in its midsection, causing it hurl over. With another shot, Dez slammed the rock solid barrel of the bat into its face, smashing it and splattering bits of yellow bone and decomposed flesh across the section of the church parking lot.

"Whew, there you go," Dez said while hunching over, catching his breath. He looked over at Professor Ulrich, who was wiping blood off his black suit jacket. "Thanks, Professor, that was quite a tackle back there."

The professor nodded and pointed to the church. "Let's get inside before any more of those things pop out of the woodwork." Dez spat on the ground and dragged the bat behind him as he made his way up the church steps.

Faith grappled with the front door's handle to no avail. "Shit, it's locked." She brushed her long blonde bangs out of her face and tried to open the door again. "How are we going to get in?"

Nathan motioned to Dez to throw him the bat. "I have an idea," he said after catching the black bat from his brother. He peered into a small window above the bushes that garnered the front lawn of the church. With a fast swing, the window broke.

Nathan cleared away the sharp edges that were still standing within the windowsill and tossed the bat back to Dez. "After you, go ahead."

Faith reached for Nathan's hand to help her into the lobby of the church. Chester slung Johnny over his shoulder and gently eased his friend onto the ledge. Faith grabbed his head and allowed him to lean back as Nathan picked up his legs to get him inside. The other three followed.

Professor Ulrich gripped the edge of the windowsill and hopped inside the church's lobby. It was completely dark inside, and the sound of the group making their way inside the building disrupted the serene quiet of the church.

Dez looked around to see if there was anyone hiding out in the building. He picked up a shard of glass and threw it across the two sets of pews in the main area of the church. He could hear it shatter as it landed near the large white altar near the stage.

Professor Ulrich peered over to a pine bookcase set up next to the stone bowl used for holding holy water near the double set of doors near the entrance. "Someone help me slide that bookcase over to the doors. If we can block off the main entrance, it'll make it harder for those things to get in here."

Chester looked over to the professor and nodded. "I'll help you out." He walked over to the bookcase and tapped the side of it to test it sturdiness. Looking over the six shelves, he began to toss out the various books and collections that garnered the furniture.

Chester removed a leather-bound Bible from the bottom shelf and flung it to the ground. It made a sickening thud as particles of dust coalesced into the gleaming moonlight passing through the church's windows.

The professor gripped his hands under one of the shelves and motioned for Chester to help him. Groaning as the two attempted to pick up the bookcase, Professor Ulrich could feel the muscles in his forearm began to tighten.

Nathan caught the two trying to move the bookcase, and walked over to help them out. The three could now easily move the item, and placed it directly in front of the two entrance doors.

"Do you think tipping it over on its side will make it a stronger barricade?" Nathan asked the professor. "The doors look pretty thick; I'm sure that this will be able to keep those things out of here."

Professor Ulrich closed his eyes and thought for a moment. "Sure, let's put it on its side." He threw his upper right arm into the bookcase, barely knocking it at all. "Wow, I'm getting old," he joked with a smile. "Guys, give me a hand again."

Chester and Nathan easily set the bookcase on its side, shoving it tightly against the entrance doors. Faith and Dez watched on, while Johnny could barely keep conscious while lying down in the corner of the lobby. "This fucking hurts," he moaned to the group. "What the hell is going on out there?"

Dez turned around and examined his friend. "Stay down, dude. I know it hurts, but we're going to ride this thing out until the morning." In his heart, Dez felt he was telling one of his closet friends a deliberate lie. Johnny leaned up and dragged himself to sit against the wall. He forced a smile as he looked at a poster promoting celibacy above him.

All members of the group were now speechless as they attempted to make wind of the situation. Faith huddled into Professor Ulrich's arms. "Bruce, I'm scared," she said with tears beginning to form in her eyes. "I don't want to die."

The professor looked at his ex-wife's beautiful face. The pulchritude still radiated from her deep blue eyes, even in a time where pure evil was reigning. "I'm not going to let you die, babe. We have a good-sized group here; none of us are going to let anything happen to you, Faith." He gripped her in his arms and inhaled the scent of her hair.

Dez looked over at Nathan, who was kicking one of the books that Chester had thrown from the bookcase. "Boring night, Little Nathan, don't you think?"

Nathan shrugged his shoulders and continued to kick the book on the church floor. "Listen, I'm the youngest one here and I'm the only one keeping my cool," he said while looking up the broken window in front of him. "We need to stay calm."

The sounds of police and ambulance sirens could be heard outside in the distance. Dez walked over to where Nathan had broken the window and looked out over the church parking lot. The crumpled body of the dead creature from earlier lay still near Nathan's car.

He reached into his jacket pocket for his cell phone. As his hand felt the fuzz on the bottom of the pocket, Dez realized that he had left his cell phone on the table at Ryan's Diner during the mad rush to escape. "I hope I'm not the only one without my cell phone," he said to the group.

Professor Ulrich, who had been pacing back and forth in the church lobby, reached into his pocket. The emptiness inside helped his heart to drop out of his chest. "Fuck! I must have left mine in Faith's car." He clenched his fingers into a fist.

"Mine is in my purse, which I now realize is probably still sitting in that booth back at the diner," Faith said with sad eyes, which were watery despite her attempts to hold off her tears.

Nathan shook his head as he pictured his phone sitting in his jacket pocket in the car. "I'm not making a daring attempt to run to my car unless there's someone who we know that can help us if we need them." He flipped the on switch for the lights of the church lobby, but it was to no avail. The only light protruding the darkness of the religious building was the heavy moonlight pouring in from outside.

Dez piped up and drew himself away from surveying the outside area. "Let's just face it: we're not going to call anybody. Even if we did have a phone, I'm sure whoever we know in this city is bracing themselves for their own protection against the walking dead." He leaned his head back against the wall and took a deep breath.

"He's right. We have to ride this thing out by ourselves." The professor walked over to Dez and put a hand on his shoulder. "There may not be any of them out there right now, but I'm sure there are a plenty of graves that are probably still pouring out their dead as we speak." He could not believe the words he was speaking.

Chester glanced over at Johnny's wound, which was worsening by the minute. He looked at his watch to see that it was almost 3 a.m. "There's only a few more hours to go. Chances are that if we all got here in one piece, we'll all walk out of here in the morning the same way. Or at least I'm hoping."

"For now, we all stick together," said Professor Ulrich with certainty. "We still have no absolute idea of anything that is going on out there. We don't even know if Revmont was the only area affected by the Venus transit. There are too many questions. We can stick this out."

Dez could hear soft moans coming from outside. Running over to the window, he could see a group of five or six creatures lumbering out of the street and into the church parking lot. Squinting his eyes, he could make out their disgusting decomposed faces. A shiver ran down his body as he watched their feet drag against the concrete ground.

"There's more coming," he said with a slight whisper. Dez brought a finger to his lips as the group peered at him. "I saw at least five of them out there. They're moving slow, but it was in this direction. Let's not make any noise."

Professor Ulrich brought his hand to Faith's mouth before she had a chance to say anything. "Honey, quiet. We need to be quiet," he whispered into her ear. She brought her hands to his and slid her fingers into them. Faith squeezed them tightly and buried her face in the professor's chest.

CHAPTER 22

▼

This was too much for Dez. He stared into the night. The air pouring in from the broken window seemed uncompromising and evil.

Dez left the group and walked into the main section of the church. Through the dark, he could see the layers of white altar staring back at him. He gripped the edge of the dark wooden pew and sat down, letting a deep breath out as he did so.

He remembered the last time he was in a church. It was Easter Sunday, and he could almost feel Koral's hands entwined in his as he thought back to that memorable weekend. It was the last time Dez had ever spent with that woman whom he thought he'd spent the rest of his life with.

The rest of his group was whispering in the lobby, keeping a close eye on the destruction and mayhem that was encompassing all outside. Dez closed and eyes and drifted away. This moment was too much for him to handle. The situation at hand, in a way, seemed like the next horrible thing in line to turn his life into shambles.

He had no job, no career. The love of his life had betrayed him, and now, the dead were rising to feast upon the residents of his hometown. He opened his eyes and licked his lips. It was starting to become cold inside the church.

Koral's pale legs were crossed, sitting next to Dez in the pew. He fought off the memories, but they were all too apparent inside of his head. His right hand was draped over her knee at the point where her beautiful darkened purple dress had ended. Dez could recall how joyous he had felt sitting next to her on the holiday, giving him the opportunistic chance to get closer to her family on such a day.

Koral's mother was sitting next to him, nudging him every so often and whispering in his ear. "Don't be so scared, sweetie," she had said with a smile. Although he had felt out of place, he knew that Koral appreciated the fact that her boyfriend had joined her and her family during the mass. Dez knew it meant a lot to her.

Dez could picture Koral's perfect shining smile sitting next to him at the Easter breakfast after mass. She made the experience more comfortable for him. All of Koral's mother's fellow churchgoers had introduced themselves to Dez, giving a cute laugh at his heavy Boston accent.

Koral had grabbed his hand and pulled him to the breakfast table. Dez could merrily recall leaning in and giving her a kiss on the cheek while reaching over for a wheat bagel on its tray.

Everything had gone downhill after that day. Sitting in the blackened arms of the church now reminded him of those bloodletting times. The pain, the torment and all of the tears shed after that day remained alive in Dez's heart.

Dez's mind shot back to that final ride to the airport in Koral's car. There was a tension that was stuck in between in predicted thoughts of future loneliness. He knew it would be another two months before he could embrace his girlfriend once again, however, he had no idea how much she would devastate his heart not even a week after that last day together.

At the airport, Koral informed Dez that she wanted her blue teddy bear back. She had given it to him at the beginning stages of their relationship; a mark or reminder of how deep the love they had shared meant.

When she had asked him if she could keep the aged and torn apart bear, Dez felt a small strike sneak into his heart. It was quickly shoved away when she placed the bear into his hands and led him to the elevator into the airline gate to catch his flight back home.

In his mind after the breakup, Dez questioned himself as to what he would have done if he had truly known that the encounter would be his last with Koral. What would he have said to her in person? What could he have possibly let out of mouth and into the deep distance of her big blue eyes?

Dez would never again make love to Koral. The last time in which he done so was stuck inside the dark recesses of his mind, playing over and over again in a mindless loop of teasing torture.

He could nearly feel himself slide into Koral, penetrating her and sensing her smooth legs wrap around his behind. His pelvis pulsating into her, she reached upon to lick his bottom lip and then bite it as she moaned with delight. Dez let himself climax, as he had always done, and let out an "I love you" before curling up into her chest, feeling her large breasts against his sweaty forearm.

Dez snapped back into the reality of the moment when Nathan and Professor Ulrich entered and sat down next to him in the pew. Nathan put a hand on his older brother's chest and looked into his eyes.

"They still haven't noticed that we're holed up in here," Nathan said. "We just realized that you were in here." Nathan adjusted his navy blue baseball cap and put his feet up on the back to the pew in front of him.

Professor Ulrich sighed and looked over at Dez. "I don't want to be the negative one of this group, but it is only a matter of time before we're going to have to fight for our lives." He breathed in and closed his eyes. "Right now, it's a game of survival. Johnny's not doing too well, either."

Dez stared straight ahead into the darkness. "Professor, I don't know what to say. I'm really messed up right now; I honestly can't believe the shit that is going down tonight." He looked up at crucifix that was hanging from the wall behind the altar at the head of the church. "These past two months have seemed like one big fucking test of patience for me. And I have a feeling it's not going to end anytime too soon."

The professor nodded and put a fist into Dez's knee. "Keep your head up, brother. We're going to make it through this. I know you've been going through a lot lately, Dez, but I'm in the same boat." He was thinking of Faith, who was sitting against a wall in the church lobby, looking after Johnny. "Let's keep our minds focused on this. We're not going to let those creatures get us tonight."

Dez blew air through his lips and nodded in agreement. "I'm sorry for ditching out on you guys. It's just this church; it's making me think too much and not adding anything positive to the situation."

Nathan kicked a church flyer that was lying on the ground in front of him. "I can't fucking believe that we don't know what's going on out there. This shit could be spreading across the country and we would have absolutely no idea." He leaned back in the pew and twisted his hat to the frontwards position.

"You're right, Nathan," Dez said to his younger brother. "It could be just Revmont, or it could be a lot more than that. Hopefully the old man's theory about the invasion ending when the transit ends is right, because we're all going to be screwed if there's thousands of walking corpses terrorizing this city in the morning."

Professor Ulrich thought of Dane, and hoped in his mind that his assistant was somewhere safe, away from the chaos. He stood up and patted Dez on the back before leaving the room.

Dez followed suit and motioned for Nathan to follow him back into the church lobby. After walking into the room, he caught a glimpse of Johnny. His friend was sitting in the corner, drifting in and out of consciousness as Faith stroked his spiky hair, trying to keep up his morale. His wound had turned nearly jet black as the other bits of blood had stained his clothes.

Faith got up and placed Johnny's head against the wall. "He's not looking very good," she said. "It seems like that bite from that monster that attacked him planted a sickness in his system. Normally, a deep cut like that wouldn't leave him so pale. In the light, I could see yellow under his eyes." Faith put her head down and coughed. "Pretty soon, he's going to go into shock and there's nothing we can do from stopping that."

Dez flinched in emotional pain and rammed his fist into the wall. The pain took a few moments to settle into the bones in his knuckles and hand. "I feel so useless!" he screamed before kneeling down next to his injured friend.

"You might want to keep your voice down, dude," Chester spurted out from his place near the window. He pointed out into the church parking lot with his mouth and jaw sealed tightly, clenching his teeth together before the rest of the group walked over to the area.

Nearly 30 members of the walking dead had found their way into the parking lot, lumbering slowly towards Nathan's car. Some were dressed in modern-day clothing, others looked like they had existed well over half a century ago. Their decayed faces and dripping skin presented the likes of an apocalyptic army heading straight for the group.

Faith held on to Professor Ulrich's arm and rested her head against his shoulder. With a dumbfounded look, he closed his eyes and for the first time of the evening, he felt completely and utterly defenseless against the terror of the night.

"It's a miracle those bastards haven't caught on yet that there's some fresh meat locked up in this church," said Chester with a sarcastic laugh. "We're stuck in here without weapons or anything that we can protect ourselves with." He leaned his head against the wall and looked at his watch.

Chester could feel himself feeling sick. It had been hours since he last had a meth fix, and the withdrawal had done a number on his body. The unnerving situation at hand was not making him feeling any better. "Professor, how the hell can something like that Venus transit cause something so drastic?" he asked, trying to shove away the pain in his torso.

Professor Ulrich glanced at the dead, who were plodding towards the church. He tried his best to be stern, but the realm of clueless entry was the only feeling he could exhibit. "I really don't know, Chester. The Venus transit might have caused a rift between our dimension and the dimension of the dead, which I'm hoping is the answer, because there might be a chance that as soon as that planetary alignment breaks, so does the dead's newfound habit of returning to life."

The group was shocked into an alert state as a loud bang was heard from further inside of the church. The sound of creaking wood soon filled the large main room of the church. "What the hell was that?" asked Nathan aloud.

Dez turned around to investigate. Walking over to the hallway entrance to the church's main room, he flipped on the light switch. The lights did not turn on. Nathan crept up behind his brother and looked over his shoulder.

"I'm going to go over there and look," Nathan said, stepping in front of Dez. With the black baseball bat in his hand, he slowly stepped up the area between the two sets of pews. Dez grabbed his arm and would not let go.

"Don't you dare go over there alone." Dez tightened his grip on Nathan's arm. "I am not going to let anything happen to you."

Nathan shoved off his brother and continued walking towards the originating spot of the noise. The two could still hear the wood panel beneath the church's altar creaking with horrific delight.

Faith, Chester and Professor Ulrich stood in the hallway's entrance. Dez looked back at them and put his right hand up, as to stop them from continuing on into the room. "Stay right there, Nathan and I are going to check it out," he said while clenching a fist.

The professor tilted his head back and led the others to the safety of the church lobby.

Nathan had already made it halfway to the area of the altar, although it was still unapparent as to what was creating the creepy noise. "Slow down, bro, slow down," said Dez, who had caught up with him and pulled lightly on his brother's shirt.

"Shut up," Nathan said as he edged closer to the altar. He placed the edge of the bat on the elevated step of the altar's stage, and followed it with his right foot. Bringing his other foot onto the stage, he himself had placed pressure on the aged wood, causing it to lightly screech.

Dez made his way up to the stage behind Nathan, and peered over the altar, but could not see anything. The only light provided was that of the moon, which was still shining through in from the many colored glass windows which garnered the walls of the giant room. The delectable moonlight was the antithesis of the terror of the night.

Nathan tapped the edge of the altar with the bat. He could hear or see nothing. Suddenly, out of the dark area of the altar, a hand grabbed Nathan's leg and forced him to the ground. The bat dropped to the ground, and Dez turned to the action.

The creature's face revealed bits of its face bone, including some of its teeth, which seemed to be falling out. Whatever was left of this man was starting to decay, as maroon slices of flesh were hanging off his cheekbones, dripping with a dark liquid that had spilled over the white sheets of the altar.

Dez grabbed the bat, but before he could swing, he was jostled to the wooden floor, sending the weapon a few feet away from him. The creature leaned down and gripped its cold, bloody hands around Nathan's neck, squeezing with brute force.

Strings of abhorrent muscle were bursting through the creature's black jacket as it tightened its grip around Nathan's throat. Gasping for air, Nathan peered into the force's black eyes, as if it had no soul. Kicking and fighting, he attempted to release himself from the thing's clutch.

"Let go of me!" shouted Nathan whilst gasping for large, panic breaths of the stale church air. His legs were violently jerking back and forth while the enemy drooled its slimy liquid from the remaining portions of its mouth.

Dez sprang to his feet and felt his tightly clenched fist strike the back of his brother's attacker. The punch did not seem to affect the living dead creature in front of him, as it continued its potent stranglehold on Nathan.

Dez let out a muffled growl as he searched for the bat. Finding it a few feet away from the battle, he lurched for the weapon and wound up for an attack on the monster.

"Here you go!" he screamed as he poured every inch of muscular power in his arms into a swing with the bat. The wood connected with the creature, who let out a haunting snarl of pain as large bits of pine forayed into the altar area.

Dez's eyes widened in shock in from the attack. Nathan reached for his own throat, which had two large mangled handprints garnering it. He coughed, letting small spools of blood quickly drip on the church's waxed stage.

The attacker rose from the ground, setting its darkened eyes on Dez, who had kneeled down to help his brother. It leaped at him, bringing its cold flesh against Dez's chest, which had been heaving in and out from loss of breath.

"Shit!" scowled Dez as he attempted to loosen the hold of the creature. He felt its sour breath grace the innards of his ear.

Nathan spat out more blood and picked up a sharp chunk of wood from the broken baseball bat. He gripped it with his fist and launched towards the monster.

With a sickening splice, the jagged portion penetrated the attacker's skull, sending droops of grey brain matter into the air. Both Nathan and the creature fell backwards into the hardened copse of the altar.

Nathan tried to move the heavy corpse on top of him, which appeared to revert back to a dead-like state. Dez leaned over and slid it on its back before giving a hand to his brother, who coughed and allowed his brother to lift him back up.

Dez kicked the creature and heard nothing in return; a sure sign that it had been defeated. He looked over at Nathan, who had once again patted the red area around his neck's skin.

"Jesus, my throat fucking hurts Dez," Nathan said as he felt around for any other wounds the living dead attacker might have inflicted.

Dez threw an arm around his brother. "I guess I should thank you for sinking that shattered piece of baseball bat into it's head, little bro." He forced a smile and playfully knocked off Nathan's baseball cap.

"I have a feeling we have a long night ahead of us." Nathan quickly sunk into a sullen mood. "Dez, one of those monsters gave us trouble. Just imagine if 30 or 40 of them burst through that front door and charged ahead?"

Dez nodded in approval. "I know, Nathan. The rest of this night is a matter of survival, and nothing more, just like the professor said. We don't even know for sure that once the transit is over that the chaos will end. I feel it might just be wishful thinking."

Nathan took in a deep breath and slid his brother's arm off his shoulder. He began to walk back to the others. Halfway through the set of pews, Chester ran up to him. He had a mildly volatile look upon his pale face.

"More of them have gathered in the parking lot. Faith saw a Revmont police car speed past without its sirens on. Jesus, what the hell happened to you two?" Chester put his hand near Nathan's reddened neck area. "That doesn't look so swell; are you alright?"

Nathan nodded before letting out a small cough. "We were attacked by one of those creatures near the altar. It had a pretty tight grip around my neck, but Dez and I fought it off."

Dez had made his way over to the two. He leaned against one of the pews, letting his hand skim the outline of a cross that was laden into the side of the pine. "I'm surprised you guys didn't hear all of the commotion. Do me a favor and make sure that his neck is going to be okay. I'm going to see how the others are doing."

Chester closely examined the handprints on Nathan's neck area. He gently felt around for any cuts. "That thing got you pretty hard, dude. If it had held on any longer, not only would it have broken your windpipe, but it would have snapped your neck bone clean in half." He removed his fingers from the examination.

Nathan shot Chester a bitter look of fearful despair.

CHAPTER 23

▼

Professor Ulrich glanced at the hordes of the undead in front the church. Their numbers were growing; soon, he thought, they would begin to creep into the safe haven in which he and his friends were hiding out.

He looked over at Faith, who was huddled in the corner of the lobby with Johnny. His bite wounds were at their most severe; it was only a matter of time before he slipped into the slow demise of death.

The professor walked over to the rest of the group, who were for the most part silent. Dez entered the lobby and immediately knelt down near his wounded friend. He placed a hand over Johnny's black spiky hair and let out a massive sigh of despair. Dez knew that he would probably not survive the remainder of the evening.

Faith nestled Johnny's head in her arms and quietly urged him to stay with her. "We're not letting you go, spiky-head. You have a group here who loves you." He didn't reply.

She turned to her ex-husband. "Bruce, he's slipping away. I don't know how much longer he's going be able to live if we don't get him to a hospital." Tears started to well in her large blue eyes.

"We can't stay here anymore," Professor Ulrich said with a sincere tone, walking over to his ex-wife. "This is merely insane. It's only a matter of time before they're in here and we all are either torn to shreds or…dead."

Dez shot the professor a look of confusion. "Professor, we do not have much of a choice here. Look it at out there; do you really think any of us stand a chance against an undead army like that?" He shook his head and looked away.

Chester stepped forward. "Dez is right. We all saw how bad it was back at the diner. Not to mention the fact that we don't know how bad the rest of the city looks," he said.

Professor Ulrich spit on the church lobby floor. He looked over at Faith, whose concern was over the declining health of their new friend. A decision had to be made. There was no way that he would allow himself and the others to waste away in the darkened church.

"We have to find medical help for Johnny," he started, with a quick shake of his fingers. "He won't survive the night; I think Faith and I should head out there into the mess and take him to a hospital. For all we know, there could be emergency stations set up on the other side of the city." He let out a deep breath.

Nathan leaned silently in the corner of the lobby. His eyes were fixated on the moonlight shining directly above and reflecting abound the chaotic creatures lumbering outside the front steps of the church in the parking lot.

Dez puffed angrily and stared directly into the professor's eyes. "Professor, from the moment I met you I could tell that you were not only a highly respectable man, but a diligently intelligent one as well. Heading out there is suicide; we have no fucking clue of how bad of shape Revmont is in right now."

The professor took a few short steps and was quickly touching torsos with Dez. He licked his lips in frustration. "I am not allowing Faith and Johnny, albeit any of us, to wait and die in this shithole. Your friend will die if we don't find help for him soon. It looks as if he has already gone into shock. I'm willing to take the risk because I am not dying in this church tonight." He stepped away from Dez.

Faith wiped away her tears and eased Johnny's body against the wall. "Bruce is right. I'm sorry, guys, but Johnny needs help or he will die in a matter of hours. I understand that you think it's best to stay put in what feels safe right now, but I cannot feel enough in my heart that I refuse to die in this place." She stood up and gripped Professor Ulrich's arm, clenching it tightly.

Dez placed his head against the side of the church's main room entrance. He glanced at Johnny, a person in which he befriended for what was now almost a decade. He remembered all of the amazing times they had together.

Dez could picture Johnny's devious grin on a night out in Boston, barhopping and having a blast.

The two were always considered the Mick Jagger and Keith Richards of the group, eliciting raucous rock 'n' roll behavior together from the moment they became friends in middle school.

Dez clearly pictured the best times the two had in and around Revmont. He remembered one night on Revmont Beach last year, where the two were sipping beers and leaning against the concrete wall which separated the sand from the parking lot.

"It's really funny," Johnny had said, his black bandanna spurring a wealth of waxed, spiked hair. "All of these instances have passed us by. We're adults now; people ready to conquer that rough world out there." He laughed and took a gulp of his drink. "We're college graduates, my friend, and I have nothing else to say."

Dez laughed and toasted the occasion. "Man, who would have thought so many years ago that we'd both be sitting here right now, gabbing about just finishing college." He knew that the two had been through so much together: lost loves, breakups, drugs, drinking and everything in between.

That cool summer night encompassed Dez's body as he drifted back into the reality of the scene. He never would have thought he'd have to say goodbye to one of his best friends. Especially not in an apocalyptic occasion as the one he and his group were facing on this particular June evening.

He fought off the salty discharge of his eyes watering and sighed. Dez wanted to be strong; his little brother was sitting not even five feet away from him. He decided that he was not going to fight the professor on the newfound decision.

"We should leave now," the professor said to Faith. "The quicker we move, the better off we'll be." He motioned to his ex-wife, who nodded in agreement.

Dez walked over to Professor Ulrich and stuck out his hand. "I want to wish you the best of luck, Professor. I respect your decision to leave. Take care of my best friend, he needs you now. Please be careful."

The professor smiled and gripped Dez's outstretched hand, nodding to his new friend. "Thank you, Dez. I'm sure we'll meet up sometime soon. I'm guessing the next time U2 tours," he said with a laugh.

Chester followed suit and shook the professor's hand. Nathan reached into his pocket and pulled out his car keys. The metallic sound of each key jingling as it is thrown into the air is ominous.

Faith tightly hugs Chester, kissing him on the cheek. She does the same for Nathan and Dez. "Pray for Johnny. We're going to do the best we can," she says to the group.

Dez and Chester begin to move the barricade away from the double doors at the church entrance. Professor Ulrich slings Johnny over his shoulder, grunting in the process. "Make sure you guys close it back up as soon as we're out of here."

Nathan patted the professor on the back. "Please, Professor, don't fuck up my car, okay?" he joked.

Professor Ulrich smiled as the barricade was lifted from the entrance to the church lobby. The smell of the dead quickly enveloped the surrounding air, forcing its way into the building.

"Run, Faith, run!" the professor shouted as they ran towards Nathan's car in the parking lot. Faith jogged past a group of monsters that were slow to realize that fresh meat had passed them by. They jabbed in her direction, but their outstretched scraggly arms missed their mark.

Professor Ulrich was slower to make it Nathan's vehicle; the added weight of Johnny on his back proved to be a major burden. Faith made it to the black Mustang first, opening the back door so the professor could ease Johnny into the backseat.

Faith screamed as a creature tugged at her blonde hair, nearly sending her backwards to the concrete ground of the parking lot. She tried her best to fight off the attacker, but more soon joined the fray.

Professor Ulrich's fist connected with one of their faces, with drips of blood and shattered yellowed teeth hurled across the air. He picked up Faith and shoved her into the car, pushing her aside as he hopped into the driver's seat.

With a turn of the key, the engine roared, alerting the entire undead army in the church parking lot. Before the professor could shift the vehicle into drive, a rambunctious attacker lunged at the front of Nathan's car, sending a loose hand into the windshield, shattering it on impact and sending shards of glass scattered across Professor Ulrich and his ex-wife.

Chester, Dez and Nathan viewed the spectacle from the two large church windows in the lobby, feeling useless and unable to help. Dez closed his eyes in terror.

*   *   *   *

Faith climbed into the backseat of the car, her long blonde bangs falling in front of her face. The sound of the electronic locks clinching was barely audible amongst the dreadful moans of the undead.

Faith lifted Johnny's head from the cushion of the backseat and placed it in her lap when she settled in. She let out a loud sigh as Professor Ulrich ferociously led the car out of the jammed parking lot.

The professor attempted to avoid the evil faces staring him down, but could not help to gaze into their black, soulless eyes. Each one represented a life that thrived at one point, perhaps living happily in the real world of Revmont before passing on to the afterlife in any manner of death.

Now, these monsters symbolized the worst fears of the human race. There was no sense of logic, no sense of reason. Their vehement faces were fixated on the darkest of the dark, now existing merely because of a dimensional shift, breathed back to life the moment Venus aligned with the sun and the earth.

These undead creatures served no purpose other than the horrid destruction of humans, tearing apart and feasting upon their flesh to quench some everlasting otherworldly hunger.

Professor Ulrich turned away to focus on the road ahead of him. He could not help but speed up, sending the car into the sides of some of the monsters, blood spurting onto the windows.

Faith kept her head down, avoiding the massacre at hand. As the professor turned the vehicle out of the church parking lot, the chaos in front of him was all too clear. Revmont's Town Square, just a half mile down the road, looked to be in mayhem and shambles. Cars were flipped over to their side and roofs, with flames bursting out of every corner.

The undead were now in control; their cold, deathly grip was now favored over the few humans left in the area. The professor caught a glimpse of an older woman with gray hair, running for her life as three zombies tackled her. The largest one of the group reached down and ripped her facial skin from the bone and immediately placed the soft flesh into its mouth.

The car was stopped in the wake of the dismay in front of them. Faith slowly turned her head to the right, Johnny's head still in her lap. One of the undead creatures was kneeling in front of a convenience store, its head buried in its arms, only coming up for air, blood drooling from its mess of a mouth.

Faith looked closer. The creature was sinking its teeth into the meaty tissue of a human arm, arteries and veins popping up from the cut, still dripping fresh blood amongst the monster's decayed hands.

CHAPTER 24

▼

Dez began to hum the opening lines of Blue Oyster Cult's "Astronomy," carefully glancing outside to the hoards of the undead, waiting for their opportunity to strike upon the three members of the group locked inside the church.

"Clock strikes midnight and moon drops burst," Dez began to sing. "...and most of you have gone away, yeah, gone away." Nathan bobbed his head in tune.

Chester shook his head at the sight of Professor Ulrich firing away with Faith and Johnny, leaving a burst of energy that alerted the ever-growing army of creatures in the church parking lot.

"Two doors locked, ten windows barred," Dez continued to sing. "One door left to take you in...the other one just mirrors in." He lightly tapped his hand against the window, a depressed look locked upon his tired face.

"A light that never warns," Chester chimed in, continuing the lyric and staring at the heavy moonlight in the air. He kicked the barricade and eased himself down to a sitting position on the floor.

Nathan, playing with a pile of pamphlets at the main entrance, threw them to the ground. The sound of fluttering paper drowned the group's thoughts. "I'd rather kill myself then let one of those undead assholes tear a chunk out of my stomach," he said, staring blankly at the ground.

A loud bang arose the three out of their respective dazes, with Chester jumping up in a ready-to-strike position. Dez walked over to the window. It finally happened; the zombies had figured out what was housed in the aging church structure.

"Shit, when they left with Johnny, they must have given off our location," said Chester, whose gaze was stuck on what looked to be a decaying older man, relentlessly banging on the front church doors, moaning in horrid hunger.

"Those are not the same ones that have been in the parking lot for the past hour," Dez said with a tone of urgency. He thumped on the barricade, testing its durability. "These bookcases are not going to be able to handle 40 or 50 of those things."

The banging outside grew louder.

"If more of those rush the front door," Chester began, "they're going to get in here pretty fucking quickly." He took several deep breaths and wiped a bead of sweat from his brow.

Nathan looked around the lobby, then focused his attention back on the sight outside of the window. "We have to draw back," he said. "If there's a basement in here, we'll have to hide out there. There's even the possibility of escaping through there, I'm hoping." He walked over to Dez, who was now staring into the lobby's small mirror.

His eyes bloodshot and face pale, Dez tried his hardest to look through the mirror, searching for a reason to justify the mortality test he and his friends were facing. He studied the bags under his eyes, analyzing them. Nathan draped his arm around his brother, embracing him in this time of survival.

"We've got no choice but to drop back," Chester stated. "It's only a matter of time before we're fighting for our lives in this lobby. Although I agree with the professor of being sick of hiding and waiting to die here...we have to move." The sweat grew on his forehead; the itch would not sustain, although in the back of his mind he felt that he had tasted his last drops of meth a while earlier in the night.

The three are startled when the sound of wood cracking is heard, along with the barricade shifting. It was time to draw back into the recesses of the church.

"Chester, let's move," Dez said sternly, looking over at his friend. Chester was staring outside the window. The masses had grown; there appeared to be well over a hundred creatures swaying in the parking lot, ready to strike upon the insides of the church.

Dez grabbed Chester by the back of the neck. "Now!" The three trotted into the main section of the church, casually looking inside the lengths of the pews for any weapons that could be used.

Walking past the altar, the remains of the evening's previous attacker lay scattered upon the stage, along with the faint smell of tainted meat. Dez pinched his nose and moved on.

"Look at this room, guys." Nathan was now in a small room to the side of the church's stage. The other two followed in, and immediately began to search the surrounding area, opening drawers and studying the walls.

It appeared to be perhaps the pastor's dressing room, complete with many colored robes, all of which were signaled with religious symbols and crosses. The one small window in the room revealed a few branches of a thick tree, bending back and forth in the later summer evening wind.

Chester passed by a mid-sized bronzed flag pole in the corner of the room. He stopped to look at it closer. He removed the heavy green flag, placing it gently on the rocking chair nearby, and gripped the pole with both hands, admiring the sharp point at its top.

He lost his clutch on the new weapon when the echoing of glass breaking emanated from the church lobby.

*   *   *   *

With a hefty display of fire emitted from the building connected to the convenience store just outside of Revmont Town Square, Professor Ulrich stepped down on the gas pedal to move through the chaos.

Faith's vision is still connected to the monster leaning in front the building, who had now finished its meal, throwing the bits of flesh and bone away from the scene. It did not wipe the massive smears of red from its face.

Unsure of where his destination might actually be, the professor continued to speed ahead. "The G. Whell Memorial Hospital is a few miles outside of Revmont. Maybe there's a chance we can make it there and get Johnny some help." The words did not seem concrete; they seemed like a lost dream.

Johnny's eyes began to open, and he let out a large groan of pain. He went back into a state of slumber soon thereafter. Faith shifted her weight and raised his head higher on her lap. His wound was completely black, cauterized with pieces of pale flesh in the spots where the sickness had not yet spread.

Professor Ulrich sped towards the road in front of him. He squinted his eyes to see what looked like a person standing in the middle of the street. It was not lumbering like the members of the undead masses.

As he strained his eyes to see the figure, a vehicle was vastly speeding ahead in the opposite direction. As it approached, the professor swerved to avoid a collision, however, found himself reeling in the force of the crash in near slow-motion.

The oncoming car struck the side of Nathan's car, sending it on its side, sparking as the metal doors slid across the pavement of the road. Both Faith and Johnny were strewn about the backseat of the car as it slowed down and collided with a brick building in Revmont Town Square. The crash sent pieces of the restaurant into the front end of Nathan's car.

Blood protruding from a wound in his forehead and dripping into his eyes, Professor Ulrich could barely see the events in front of him. He could make out the opposing vehicle, which had collided with a large oak tree in the square.

As he pulled an arm from the seatbelt, a stinging pain was unearthed in his chest. He used two fingers to wipe the thick blood from his vision.

As he turned his neck, he could see a group of creatures run towards the other vehicle, pulling out the driver through the broken window, to the ground. They began to tear at the man's shoulder, ripping out long strands of muscle and forcing them into hungry mouths.

The man screamed in such way that it sent chills throughout the professor's heavily bruised body. He forgot about the pain as the revulsion unfolded in his line of sight.

One of the creatures dug its hand into the man's stomach, pulling out the goopy intestines and tearing apart what looked to be one of his kidneys. The screeching stopped as more blood dripped into Professor Ulrich's eyes.

CHAPTER 25

▼

Chester picked up and clenched the bronze pole with white knuckles. Moving out of the pastor's room and onto the church stage, both Nathan and Dez followed closely behind him.

Taking small, careful steps, the group inched over to the lobby. Contained therein were five of the undead, looking around the lobby for any signs of food. Their drooling mouths open, they garnered the area with their deathly smell and putrid aroma.

Two of the zombies had pale blue faces, and Dez envisioned that they might have been freshly lain in the graveyard in recent weeks. The other three were haggard displays of decomposition, their dark flesh hanging from bits of bone matter. Their eyes had one thing in common: the soulless black of callousness.

A creature with an arm missing swung at the mirror on the wall, sending it to the ground in many pieces. The boom of the destruction was menacing, an omen of evil. Their incessant moans began to fill the once silent church.

Dez pulled on Chester's shirt in an attempt to retrieve his attention. He turned around, a blank stare stuck on his face. "There's five of them," he whispered. "Maybe more if they continue to come in through that broken window. We have to move back." He gripped the pole tighter.

Nathan poked his head up. "There was a door in the pastor's room. It might lead to the basement. If we can hide out there, it will buy us some serious time."

Dez could feel the frightened teenager in his brother. He always knew that his connection with Nathan was one of solitude's bond. Standing in the terror of the night, he knew that Nathan feared for not only his own life, but that of Dez and Chester as well.

Dez placed his hand on Nathan's side, slightly feeling his brother's newfound nervous shake. "Let's move back," he said, motioning for the group to fall back to the pastor's room. He urged the two to move slowly and quietly, for fear of alerting their attackers in the next room.

Nathan peered at the multi-colored windows that decorated the side walls of the main section of the church. As he stepped back, the moonlight became colorful and inviting, as opposed to the wickedness it has presented most of the evening.

Moving back, they were nearing the pastor's room. Nathan's fixation on the walls of the church distracted him from his steps. He bumped into Chester, who fell back and knocked over a line of candles encased in green glass.

Each one hit the church floor and smashed with an encompassing strike. The creatures in the lobby picked up their attention to the overbearing noise, trudging towards the epicenter of the shatter. They began to rage, and more of the undead filtered in through the broken window in the lobby.

Dez grabbed Chester by the front of his shirt and pulled him back up, beginning to run in the direction of the pastor's room. Once inside, Nathan quickly opened the door within, revealing a dark staircase that led to the church's dank basement.

Nathan was first to head into the shadowy abyss, followed by Chester, then Dez, who slammed the door shut behind him.

Although it was hard to trollop down the staircase without the advent of light, within seconds, Nathan's arm had struck another door. Pushing it open, he reached for the light switch and flipped it up. The click was banter of hope and appeal.

A single light bulb in the middle of the room was the area's only beacon of light besides a small amount of moonlight from a window on the opposite side of the basement. Chester immediately pointed to a large armoire standing a few feet away from the basement door.

Dez let his fingers slide underneath the dusty pine of the object, feeling years and years of dirt and grime slip underneath his short fingernails. Chester gripped the other side of the armoire and the two attempted to lift it, but failed.

"Well, I guess that's a good sign." Chester coughed in the wake of a stream of dust. "That thing is heavy. If we can push it front of the door, it could be a better barricade than the one we had upstairs."

Nathan nodded and placed himself next to Dez, who began to push the armoire in the direction of the door. As Chester pulled, the three managed to move the heft item slowly in front of the door, another barricade from the outside world of the vicious undead.

Dez let out a sigh of struggle and gently tapped the light bulb, which swung freely from side to side, its light projecting shadows of the figures amongst the damp church basement. As the three began to search for weapons and tools in the basement, the rumbling of heavy footsteps could be heard from the upstairs section of the church.

"They know we are in this church somewhere," said Chester. "I'm sure those fuckers can smell us down here." He shook his head and placed the bronze pole against the wall. He loosened his fingers and shoved them in his pants pockets.

Dez walked over to the window. He could barely see the legs of the creatures outside the church. Some were walking; others were slowly moving along, perhaps frustrated at their loss of nourishment.

He wiped the window with his hand, leaving black streaks on all of his fingers. He wiped them on this shirt and continued to gaze outside. "Here we are again," Dez said, "hiding from those monsters. I'm sick of this, and I'm sick to my stomach over how Professor Ulrich and the others are. I want to know if Johnny is alive." He closed his eyes.

Nathan leaned against an old piano that was placed against the basement wall. Spiderwebs garnered the ivory keys; it had not been used in years.

"The professor was doing his best. He wanted to make sure Johnny survived the night. I'm sure he wants to make sure that all of us survive the night," Nathan said, drawing a circle with his index finger in the center of the piano.

The zombies were franticly searching for human flesh in the main section of the church. They slowly filled the pews, some falling over as more and more began to climb through the window.

Their echoing footsteps carried through to the basement.

Nathan peered outside as he walked over to the window. "I say we jump out of here and just run. Who knows what's going on out there right now?" He poked at the window but quickly stopped.

"Exactly," said Chester. "We have no idea as to what is going on out there. We don't even know if this has spread to any other areas. Dez, do you think the professor was right in saying that all of this could end with the impending conclusion of the transit?" He looked over at his friend, who was now on his knees in the corner, searching for something.

"I really don't know, bro." Dez picked up a solid piece of heavy steel pipe. He took a practice swing and nodded. "This will do."

Nathan motioned for his brother to toss him the pipe. "Nice and thick; if one of those walking pus bags comes near you, bash it in the head and spill its brains on the wall," he said with an infuriated tone after Dez threw him the weapon.

Dez retrieved the pipe back from his brother and walked over to the window. He observed the many members of the army of the walking dead and spit on the window, letting droplets of his phlegm drip down into the perimeter. The remaining strands of his positive attitude were drained.

"We're fucked now. Johnny could be dead, as well as the professor and Faith. For all we know, they're in the stomachs of those creatures," he began, an emotional twill in his voice. "We should have never split up. I'm never going to see my best friend again. I'm not going to be able to look over at him at midnight on a Saturday and raise my glass to him."

Dez looked over at his brother, then at Chester. He pointed at each at them. "Let me tell you guys something. Death is *here.* The name of the game is survival, boys." He pointed his weapon in the direction of the barricaded door. "Once they burst through there, and I know they will, we have to *fight.*"

For some reason, Dez flashed back to the very day Koral had broken up with him. He remembered it clearly; he could replay every solitary moment of the day in his head.

The sun was shining brightly outside. The previous evening, Dez had gone out drinking with Chester and Johnny, a usual occurrence for the mid-week blues. He had noticed a slight sense of disarray in his girlfriend's voice when they talked before bedtime.

Dez could remember that she didn't sound *happy.* He shook it off and had gone to bed, a few beers rifling through his system.

The cell phone ring awoke him. He caught a glimpse of the sun and allowed himself to ease out of bed to reach for the phone. Koral had never called him this early in the morning. And when she did, it was only because she missed him and wanted to talk to him on her 15-minute drive to work.

"I'm not in love with you, Dez," Koral had said on that fateful spring morning. "I…I just don't feel the way I used to about you. My heart doesn't skip a beat when you step off that plane anymore. I'm sorry Dez, but it's over."

He remembered the wave of shock that enveloped his body, his inability to move for an hour afterwards. All he could ask her was "Why?" Her answers weren't good enough, he had told her. A lifetime of romance and happiness that he had banked on was now gone.

The days preceding the breakup were heart-wrenching. Dez spent the majority of his time in a pair of torn black jogging shorts and a white undershirt. The pain was overwhelming; there was no place he could go without experiencing a strike of remembrance in his chest.

Dez fell back on his friends. After all, they were all he had. Chester, Nathan and Johnny had tried their best to comfort him, however, it seemed like a lost cause at most times.

Dez remembered her smile, her hair, her smell; now, the hurt, the pain…it all seemed trivial. His best friend was probably dead somewhere in the city. His hometown was in shambles, destroyed by a dimensional shift in space.

Survival. Survival was the only notion of sanity left.

"I'm not dying tonight, boys," Dez said clenching the pipe in his hands. "If I have to go down taking one of those fuckers out with me, here's to hoping that there's a hell for all of us to have a few drinks." He let out a deep breath and looked out the window.

Nathan placed his head against his brother's brow. He crumpled the edge of the shoulder of Dez's shirt. "Let's do this," he said with clenched teeth.

The sound of the footsteps of the dead began to echo throughout the dank cavern of the church basement.

*   *   *   *

Faith regained consciousness and reached around to feel the warmness of her ex-husband's hand. She could feel the pain beginning to travel throughout her legs. She noticed that Johnny's head was no longer placed in her lap.

Professor Ulrich locked hands with Faith. He could feel the blood smeared against the inside of their grip. "Bruce, I love you," Faith stammered, tears beginning to stream down her face, further ruining her makeup. "I don't want to die."

The professor smiled and tried to move his body. "Baby, I love you. I promise that nothing is going to happen to you as long as I'm around." The wreckage had sent Faith's body into the front seat, her legs jammed into the dashboard.

Professor Ulrich tried hard to move his body once again. This time he was successful. "Faith, stay put, and don't make any noise. I'm going to slip out of the window and pull out you, okay?" He strained his upper body to pull himself up. When he did so, he fell to the ground and felt the broken glass under his thin suit jacket. He noticed that his U2 pin had fallen off at some point during the long evening.

The professor stayed quiet as he observed the area. Surprisingly, the amount of undead creatures had subsided, leaving a few scattered ones chowing on the remains of the other driver from the car collision.

As Professor Ulrich reached up to the vehicle to pull out Faith, bright head-lights with a bluish tint momentarily blinded his vision. He didn't see any other moving cars in the town square.

"Professor!" the voice from the headlights shouted.

"Dane!" The professor was tackled by his graduate assistant, who immediately hugged him and helped him to his feet. He pointed to Faith, and the two lifted her up. As she stepped to the ground, the pain in her legs worsened.

"Dane, my God, you're alive!" Faith grasped the assistant closely and smooched him on the cheek.

"I saw the accident from the edge of Revmont Town Square. I had been parked there earlier in the night, you know, just in case something actually happened because of the transit. Something broke my windshield and I fainted. I woke up and hour ago and saw the destruction across the square."

Professor Ulrich sighed in relief. "You're lucky to be alive, Dane. Those zombies are tearing everyone in sight apart." He looked over at the wreckage and remembered Johnny. "Where the hell did Johnny go?"

Faith suddenly screamed at the top of her lungs and fell to the ground, obviously shaken up. The professor looked down and saw the upper half of Johnny's body on the ground. Torn at the waistline, his intestines were obtruded from his body, leaving a small trail of blood and black liquid.

Professor Ulrich felt the hairs on his arms stand up, goosebumps inching from his skin in the cold horror that lay before him. He pulled Faith into his arms and turned away from the gruesome scene.

The sound of slurping was heard behind the car wreckage, followed by the crunching of bone. A creature emerged, its face bloodied with the remains of Johnny's insides, ready to strike again.

Dane picked up a piece of steel from the wreckage and shoved into the zombie's chest, hurling it to the ground. "Run! Follow me!"

After a few minutes, the three stopped at Nilsson Hardware, a hardware store at the edge of Revmont Town Square. The door kicked in, the group entered and dropped down behind the counter. Faith fell into the professor's arms as Dane stood up to look out for any new attackers.

"I don't see anymore, they must have been attracted to something further down the road. I saw a bunch of survivors run past my car when I woke up. I was confused, so I didn't say anything to them," said Dane as he searched for a viable weapon in the hardware store.

As he stepped into the back room, he felt a sticky substance grip the bottom of his Doc Marten boots. Lifting his right foot up into the air, he held his hand to his mouth to prevent himself from vomiting.

Below Dane lied the remains of the hardware store owner, his green apron torn to shreds, mingled with pieces of scattered flesh. His skull had split in two perfect V-shaped bits, allowing his brain to shift onto the cold concrete ground of the store.

Dane turned himself away from the mess, his feet nestled into the perfect allotment of blood on the floor.

CHAPTER 26

▼

The sounds of the undead footsteps subsided as soon as the banging began. Dez paced back and forth in the church basement, ready and poised for the fight ahead. In the back of his mind, he knew the next hour of his life would be pivotal.

Both Chester and Nathan stared at the window, distancing their thoughts from the noise the monsters were creating upstairs. They noticed the wave of new creatures moving towards the direction of the front entrance of the church. The army had surely gotten wind of the hopes of a massive feast contained therein.

At first, what sounded like the moving of furniture quickly unearthed the group's fear: the creatures had opened the pastor's room door that led to the basement. It was only a matter of time before they had reached the barricade at the basement entrance.

The door to the staircase creaked open, allowing a few fiends to fall freely down the stairs, ending in the sickening thud against the barricade. More and more began to pour down, and before long, they were pounding at the basement door, eager to tear down both the barricade and the humans inside.

The aging wood door creaked as the creatures continually clobbered it with their rotten, fleshy fists. Dez knew that the barricade would not last very long against the many members of the undead.

Chester could hear the incessant thumping and took a close look at the window. His eyes shot open with a lightning bolt of surprise as a small smile took over his face. He tapped Nathan on the shoulder and called out for Dez. "Guys, this is a long shot...but I may have figured out a way to for us to get out of this church through the window unscathed."

Dez tilted his side to the side in confusion. "Chester, there's got to be hundreds of those things out there. Even if we were able to get out of this immediate area, the unknown is still a factor. There could be a thousand more waiting around the corner." He leaned the pipe in his hand against the wall, making a small metallic clang.

Chester blinked quickly and shook his head. "No Dez, I think this might be a good plan." He leaned into the window, careful enough not to hit it, and pointed to a rusty water nozzle a few inches from the window pane, connected to a black emergency hose. "Of course, I realize that a heavy stream of water is not going to *hurt* them. But there's a possibility that it'll buy us a few minutes to escape if they back away. They used to do it to the lunatics back in the day." His eyed widened.

Dez tilted his head into a slight nod of agreement. "How are we sure that the water is still turned on this place? It's been closed down for over a while now."

"It's a chance, but I'm pretty sure that the city officials would not turn off the water. It's illegal to turn off an emergency fire house. Electricity, yes, but apparently they haven't even gotten to that issue yet," Chester said, pointing in the direction of the basement's lone light bulb, which was hanging perfectly still in the center of the room, creating shadows of the three characters as they planned their breakout.

Nathan stood in agreement with Chester. "He's got a good idea here, Dez," he began, giving his friend a soft high-five. "If we blast those things with some water, maybe they're either be confused or draw back. Even if it's a little, it gives a chance to make a quick run towards the other side of this church."

As Nathan ended his words, the first sounds of breaking wood filled the dank and lonely basement. The undead has begun to pounce on the door, the heavy barricade the only protection from their hungry efforts.

"We're not going to die down here, remember?" Chester looked over at Dez with strong eyes. "I'd rather die fighting in the streets of Revmont instead of inviting those monsters to a buffet down in this fucking basement."

Dez stood silent and still, pondering the plan. He knew that drastic action would be needed. More so, he knew that he and his group would need to fight for their lives. "Chester, as soon as Nathan unhinges the window, slide out and take the hose with you. Nathan, you follow and bash whoever gets in his way. I'll turn on the water and follow right behind you," he commanded, ready to accelerate his intentions with Chester's new plan for escape.

As Nathan began to unhinge the small window, one of the creature's fists burst through the thin basement door, spilling small bits of wood to the cold ground underneath. The armoire shaking, it would not be long before the outside force pushed it to the ground.

Nathan successfully opened the window. Chester slid outside, his shirt grappling onto the corroded rust around the metal window pane. Touching the pavement outside of the basement, he carefully looked up to see the hordes of the undead moving along towards the front entrance. It had appeared that none of them had seen him crawl from the window space.

Chester surveyed the surrounding area and placed a strong grip on the rusty nozzle. Nathan began to climb outside, but was startled when the weighty drawers of the armoire began to putter violently. "Nathan, keep moving!" Dez ordered, pipe in hand in case of the army's breaking of the barricade.

Nathan rolled out onto the pavement. Dez picked up the bronze flag pole from the floor and threw it to his brother, who scooped it up and immediately fronted a battle stance, eagerly waiting for Dez to throw on the vehement stream of water from the hose.

The barricade burst. The heavy armoire toppled to it side as more than 20 creatures pushed it aside. Their load moans broke the crisp, dull air of the church basement.

Dez turned on the water and jumped through the window, parts of his shirt hooking onto the window pane. He jerked the fabric from the steel and brought his weapon through the space, leaving the church basement.

Chester pulled the nozzle and felt the water rise into the hose, streaming its way towards the opening. A few creatures whom had seen the act began to make their way towards the scene, followed by others who were startled upon the escape of the three.

Chester stood back and braced himself for the force, spurting the rapid flow of water in a forward direction, wetting the group of monsters nearing the group. Some confused, they threw their hands up towards their faces, unknowing of what to do. Others were thrown back.

A zombie burst through the stream of water and lunged at Dez, who brought his pipe to the air and let it smack the skull of the creature, immediately sending it to the pavement. The thud was followed by another walloping, as Dez continued his attack until the corpse lay lifeless on the ground.

Water soaking their tattered clothing, some of the undead began to back away from the three, allowing Chester to stand in front of his friends and continue the stream of liquid. Dez and Nathan backed him, fighting off the few creatures who were unaffected by the aqueous assault.

"Keep moving back! The hose is about thirty feet long, it should be enough for us to slip out through those bushes on the side of the church!" screamed Chester, feeling the cold water drench his pale, clenched hands.

Nathan grabbed the back of Chester's shirt, pulling him in the direction he and Dez were moving as the hose continued to spray. Dez's pipe collided with the face of a corpse who had pulled him to the side. Muscles blazing, he swung with all of his strength, sending the creature's facial bones in flight and spilling blood on his arms.

During the fracas, a 7-foot creature grabbed Nathan, pulling him from the fray. As he attempted to fight back, he was not able to get a clear swipe with the flag pole. The undead attacker sunk its teeth into Nathan's shoulder, tearing out a generous portion of flesh.

With a scream of unbearable pain, Nathan freed himself from the monster's grasp, falling to the ground. He grabbed the flag pole and brought his arm back to launch it, keeping footing on the concrete pavement below him. The pole flew a few feet into the air until it struck the zombie, its pointy bronze tip lodged directly in its right eye socket. The black of its pupil began to drip around the wound, followed by loads of pulpy blood.

Nathan put a hand over his new wound and bumped into Chester, who was rapidly running out of hose length during his continuous spray of the army. Dez caught wind of his brother's injury and pulled Chester towards the running direction. "Chester, move!" Dez shouted as he felt a grip of chill embrace his body.

Chester dropped the hose as the undead horde relinquished its drawback, shaking the icy water from their torsos and regaining their sense of urgent ghastly feeding.

Dez was the first to reach the thick, green shrubbery surrounding the opposite end of the church. He immediately clutched Nathan and helped him move along. Chester inched down to take a breath, the mass of the undead now far behind them, unaware of where their prey had wandered.

Dez reached down and grabbed part of the bush below him, breathing in and out after the ordeal of escape. His vision caught the thick amount of blood protruding from his brother's bite wound. "Chester, look at Nathan's shoulder," he said calmly.

Chester, his lungs heaving from the attack, opened his eyes and placed a hand on Nathan's shoulder, who winced in pain upon the touch. Chester analyzed the gash, gently running his finger along side the spots where the creature had torn away bits of Nathan's flesh. "It's a deep wound, and may be worse than the one Johnny suffered. That asshole must have dug its teeth pretty far in; there's a pretty good chunk of skin missing from his shoulder," Chester stated as he wiped away some of the blood from the area.

Dez spat and clenched his fist. "Motherfucker! I should have cracked that thing in the skull before it got a chance to attack you." Looking down, he felt a sense of failure envelop his thoughts, followed by the terror of uncertainty over the group's future.

Nathan reached his hand over to his brother's and felt the uneasiness in his fingertips. "Dez, it's okay. That monster was probably well over seven feet tall. It just reached down and grabbed me without a problem." He turned his head to the side as the throbbing grew worse.

Dez peered at the wound, then brought his eyes to the area in which the group had just tread, wondering if the undead had gotten notice of where his group was now hiding. Stepping in a puddle underneath the bush, he brought his attention to a nearby construction site, which from the distance seemed to be uninhabited.

"That's where the city is starting to build a new condominium complex," said Chester, catching his friend's line of sight. "I think we'll be a hell of a lot safer there than hiding out in these bushes." He clutched his chest, catching more of his breath. "Let's make our move over there."

Dez patted Nathan on the head. He knew his brother was in an extreme amount of pain, yet still remained optimistic about their situation. He looked at Chester, his brown hair strewn in various directions. He felt for their group; the night had taken yet another turn for the worst.

Dez wondered aloud where the professor, Faith and Johnny might be. "I'd kill to find out where they are," he said. "Our best friend could be dead right now, and we wouldn't know." He looked behind him; he could see the undead beginning to trek their way to the group's newfound hiding spot.

With Nathan leaning against his side, Dez motioned for Chester to follow him to the construction site. Dez could feel the blood flowing out of his brother's bite wound. The warm dribble only infuriated him more and more. For a moment, he pictured himself in bed at his apartment, sleeping while the bright sunshine poured in through his window.

"Dez! Dez!" Chester was shouting. "Look." He pointed to the massive structure in front of them. The basis of what would be the condominium complex had been laid out; the rigid steel beams were in place, flanked by various instruments of construction equipment.

Each steel beam of the structure was lined with strings of light bulbs. Oddly, they were all on, illuminating the complex.

Large puddles garnered the hard ground underneath them. Dez stepped off a muddy piece of grass, leaving the large imprint of his boot. Nathan's weight was forcing his body to shift, he had to stop and regain his footing before moving onto the site.

Dez stopped at a massive wooden workbench as they neared the condo structure. He leaned Nathan against the panel and plopped down onto the ground. "I can't believe that there is not a single, solitary zombie out here. It's only a matter of time before they find us here. What the fuck are we going to do, Chester?" Dez's voice was pinched with bits of fright.

Chester hung his head in disbelief. He didn't know what to do in this situation. Placing his arm against the workbench, he glanced at Nathan's wound, which had finally stopped bleeding. "First off, we have to arm ourselves," he said, picking up a two-foot long metal rod near his foot.

A vociferous blast cut off the rest off Chester's words. Looking over above the hill that connected the construction site to the rest of Revmont, all that could be seen was fire. An explosion had rocked the area, but none of them knew what the cause could be.

Dez's focus was unaffected by the loud blast. "I'm not surprised to see something like that. It either gives me hope that there are other survivors fighting these monsters off, or reinforces my belief that this will be the last night any of us will spend on this earth." His brown eyes reflected the wavering fire in the distance.

Amidst Nathan's heavy breathing, the group remained quiet. Chester gripped the metal rod, still confused as to what to do next. Nathan's hand was locked over his wound, which had started to turn a repulsive dark color as it appeared to grow worse.

Dez placed his hands together in a prayer position, letting the top section of fingertips to rest against his lips. Life before this June evening seemed trivial; pining over Koral meant nearly nothing to him at this point. He looked up to the sky to see the moon, which remained full and bright.

The menacing light from the strings of bulbs among the unit's beams was now mirrored off the three pale faces in the night.

CHAPTER 27

▼

Buried in Professor Ulrich's arms, Faith cowered at the sight of what appeared to be the remains of the hardware store owner on the cold concrete floor.

The smell of lumber and paint was now mixed with the subsequent smell of death. The professor could feel the chill take hold of his body as his ex-wife locked herself in his arms. He could tell she was still crying; the soft, wet tears ran right through his suit jacket.

Professor Ulrich immersed himself in the warm memories of the past. He remembered one of his first vacations with Faith. Northern Boston University was on spring break, and he and Faith decided that a trip to Florida would help the couple unwind and relax before heading back to the real world.

Faith, decked out in a dark green bikini, nestled herself in Professor Ulrich's chest. He could almost feel the dewy tropical air sticking to their bodies, the faint smell of sex on the horizon.

"Bruce, this feels so right," Faith had said, sand caressing their bodies as they lied on the beach, worries drifting away with the tide. "I love you so much." She reached over and let her hand glide over his chest.

They had slept on the beach that night, allowing the quiet night and their close embrace to accompany their dreams. Professor Ulrich remembered waking up next to her the next morning, at that point realizing that he wanted to sleep next to Faith for every night of the rest of their lives.

Things were much different now, and the divorce was one of the last things on his mind. The professor, Faith and Dane were amid a fight for the lives. What had started as an awkward night became the most deviated terror of their existence.

Scattered moans outside the store flinched the professor back into consciousness. He sat restless, wondering as to what would unfold next in the course of the evening. He knew that they were not safe in the hardware store; soon the creatures would find them.

Faith lifted her head off of the professor's shoulders. Wiping away her tears, she glanced outside at the carnage. Although she felt safe in the comfort of Professor Ulrich's arms, she longed for a return to normalcy. She longed to return to the recess that was the beginning part of the evening.

Dane sat across from the two, his blue sneakers just inches away from the pool of blood from the insides of the hardware store owner. His eyes were focused on the window in the front section of the store. He seemed to be waiting for the chaos to enter the building, although he knew deep inside neither one of them was ready to handle a massive attack.

He looked over at the professor, whose face had blood streaks from the preceding car accident, and his eyes were staring at the floor.

Professor Ulrich finally lifted his head and glanced at Dane before giving Faith a kiss on the top of her head. He wiped back her hair and sighed. "Dane, what does it look like out there?"

Dane shifted his position from the floor and slowly crawled to where the professor and Faith were sitting. He edged his head just above the counter, peeking about to gauge whatever chaos was awaiting outside the hardware store.

One creature was kneeling outside the front of the store. It appeared to be moving unhurriedly, its head positioned as if it were eating something. Dane could see the smears of blood on the monster's cheeks as it chewed on a rough piece of human flesh. It brought its head up only when scattered noises entered the encompassing area.

Dane slid back down to where the professor and his ex-wife were sitting. "There's only one of them out there," he whispered. "I couldn't see anything else. I hope that maybe the majority of them have moved on to other parts of the city so we can get out of this hiding spot." He adjusted the tongue on his sneakers and tilted his back against the counter.

As he put his hand down, his fingers scraped a large mallet lying on the ground. Dane picked it up and examined it, putting his right hand above his left while taking a small practice swing.

Professor Ulrich began to sit up, letting go of his grip on Faith. She leaned back and reached for his cheek, running her finger alongside it, smiling. The professor returned the gesture and immediately went in for a lengthy kiss. "I love you," he said, bringing his mouth back, their lips disconnected from their quick clinch. "We're not doing to die tonight, Faith. I'm not going to let it happen to us."

The professor then looked over to Dane and punched his knee. With a nod, he outstretched his hand and gripped Dane's hand, shaking it with vigorous glory. Their grip was tight, perhaps signifying the two's close professional relationship, which in recent weeks had reached high levels of respect.

Dane's eye caught a crowbar lying next to the remains of the hardware store owner. His blue sneaker making a perfect imprint in the pool of blood, he snatched the crowbar and tossed it to the professor, who caught it with one hand.

Veins attempting to protrude through his arm muscles, Professor Ulrich took both hands to the crowbar. All of the anger, all of the unjust inevitability of the horror the evening echoed through his brain; he had never thought his life would have come to down to this fight for survival. And he certainly had never thought he would be exchanging those three simple words with Faith ever again in his lifetime.

One moan turned to many in a matter of minutes. The horde of the undead were approaching, perhaps startled by a human survivor passing by the middle section of Revmont Town Square.

Faith once again wrapped her arms around the professor, who took a hand off of the weapon to squeeze her fingers. She buried her face in his back, smelling the final remnants of his cologne from the evening. Faith inhaled the sweet scent, which brought her senses back to the more jovial days of their relationship.

She could remember their wedding day. The small garden ceremony was an event she considered to be the happiest day of her life. Faith thought back to the way her wedding dress felt on her, the lace gently touching her tanned legs as her bridesmaids fixed her blonde hair.

Faith could recall the sun's bright gleam against the polished wooden chairs at the small wedding ceremony. The garden was beautiful; garnered with tulips and white roses, it almost brought her to tears as the opening music was played.

Her husband-to-be was the most handsome man she had ever been with; the way his eyes looked down upon her as he read their personalized vows wowed her with extreme pulchritude. Faith loved the professor, and honestly believed she'd spend the rest of her life with him in harmonious bliss.

It wasn't until the final year of their marriage that things went sour, according to Faith. Professor Ulrich was wrapped up nearly completely in his work, and their evenings together revolved mostly around which classes he was most looking forward to teaching the following day.

At this very moment, Faith wanted to return to those moments with her man. She wanted to experience the warm times of love and happiness with the professor. She wanted to wrap her legs around him during the cold nights of the New England winter and make love to him. Most of all, she wanted an escape from the absolute terror of the events unfolding in front of her.

The moans grew louder. Dane could barely see the shadows of the oncoming assault of creatures outside the store. He clasped the wood of the mallet's base and leaned back, returning to his spot behind the counter. They would be here soon.

Dane pinched the outset of Professor Ulrich's jacket. His mentor did not even look over at him; he knew what was coming.

The professor grabbed Faith by both of her arms after setting the black crowbar on the floor. His head down, he ran his hands up and down her jean jacket. "Faith, I want you to go into the back room of the store and lock the door. Do not let anyone, or anything, in." Professor Ulrich failed to look directly into her eyes.

Faith's eyes continue to well with tears. It was hard for her to allow her words to escape. "Bruce, no! I am not going back there by myself! I don't want you or Dane to die!" Her whispering was the loudest she could have possibly performed without screaming in emotional agony.

Professor Ulrich could hear the footsteps of the zombies dragging along the pavement of the town square. Their unearthly moans were growing more voluble with each passing second. He was hoping that they might pass by the hardware store without recognizing the banquet inside.

Faith punched the professor's chest. He drew back, then nestled her inside of his arms and chest. "Faith, you have to do this for us. You have to do this for me. Dane and I are the only line of defense in here. If you're locked back there, there's a greater chance of survival." His words were all out of disbelief.

Fists clenched, she broke down and let the tears flow freely. "Bruce, please..." Her dialogue was cut off by the creatures' incessant groans. "Please don't leave me. I don't want you to die." Whatever eyeshadow remaining on her face was drooped into a dark bluish mess on her cheeks.

Professor Ulrich collected himself and backed away from Faith. He pointed in the outside direction for Dane to keep a lookout. He stepped into the back room of the store, which was littered with half-empty cans of paint and various construction tools. There was a Red Sox poster on the wall, featuring a large aerial view of Fenway Park.

The professor kicked away the paint cans, some spilling over. He pulled a large hammer off a shelf in the room and handed it to Faith, who was leaning against the counter, tears streaming from her face and dripping into her chest region.

Faith gently retrieved the hammer from Professor Ulrich and reached for his free hand. He pulled her up, embracing her in his arms before diving in for a lengthy kiss. He felt her tongue penetrate his mouth, the affectionate display seeming to be the last of its kind.

Dane could not help but watch the scene, at times feeling his mentor's pain of leaving his ex-wife. He turned his head back to looking outside the hardware store window. Shuffling his feet below him, he gripped the mallet, ready for any signs of intruders.

Professor Ulrich brought Faith to the back room and sat her down on the floor. Green paint soaking the bottom of her tight jeans, she felt the wetness but quickly ignored it. The professor kneeled down in front of her.

"I love you more than you'll ever know," he said, eyes starting to water from the sting of leaving Faith. "Stay back here, Faith. I love you."

"I love you, Bruce." Faith did not want to let go of his hand, but allowed it. The door closed, leaving her without much light. The portentous thoughts began to fill her head as the darkness took over her space.

The first member of the living dead broke the front window, sending Dane spiraling backwards. After the fall, he jumped back to his feet and met his attacker.

The creature had barely any facial skin left. It lunged for Dane's throat, but he shoved it away, ending the push with a quick swipe of his mallet. The heavy metal end connected with the zombie's chest. With a large groan, it fell to the ground among the pieces of shattered window.

Professor Ulrich removed the door handle from the back room door and joined Dane in the fray. More of the undead began to notice the fracas, and soon made their way over to the store, piling in through the broken window.

The injured monster slowly stood up, but not before Dane bashed the back of its skull with his weapon. It did not get up again.

Three creatures had now entered the hardware store. Professor Ulrich leaned back and pounced on the first one to enter the building, falling on top of it as the both of them fell to the ground.

He freed his right hand and let the crowbar fly. The cheek of the zombie was pierced as the metal gushed through the rotting flesh. Its beige teeth cracked from the blow, it continued to fight for the professor's flesh.

Dane stepped in and brought his mallet behind his back, winding up for a powerful swing. The remaining teeth split in different directions in a mess of blood and brain matter across the side of the hardware store counter.

One of the creatures hopped onto Dane's back. Before he had a chance to shrug it off his body, its teeth had already punctured the back of his head. The jolting pain rushed throughout his spine. With an enormous flip, the zombie faltered to the floor. Dane grabbed the back of his head and felt the warm ooze of blood surge through the insets of his fingers.

Blood sticking his hand to the wooden base of the mallet, Dane let his rage flow through his swings, knocking the creatures to the ground. Some suffered head shots that immediately resulted in their demise, while others continued to fight on.

The professor was locked in battle with two attackers of his own, who had cornered him off to the side of the store. Its repulsive hand on his throat, he gasped for air and to free himself from their grip. He felt around behind him franticly, picking up a small screwdriver.

Professor Ulrich jammed the screwdriver into one of his attacker's eyes and felt the mushy black portion of its eye gel around the metal end of the tool. It released its hand from his throat and fell to the floor.

"Fuck!" screamed the professor as he took in giant breaths of air. "Dane!"

Dane was caught in a tussle with one of the creatures. His gaping swings missing his target, more and more of the undead made their way into the store, much to the dismay of the two.

The ghouls ganged up on the thin-framed Dane, pushing him to the ground. One of the monsters reached for his hand and pulled away his thumb, taking a section of bone of small veins as it ripped away from the rest of the flesh. Dane screamed in agony as it brought its small meal to its mouth and began to chew.

He reached for his mallet, which had fallen as he was shoved to the ground, but it was too late to fight back. His sight was beginning to diminish. The twinge of acute pain encompassed his body. The creatures had won, and were beginning to plunge into his intestinal region, pulling out his insides, bringing the meat into their hungry mouths.

The professor watched in revulsion as his graduate assistant was torn apart, a seemingly extravagant buffet for the undead monsters. Flashes of Dane twinkled in his head, images of better times.

For a second, Professor Ulrich thought of joining Faith in the back room of the hardware store, however, did not want to cause the love of his life to perish along with himself and Dane. There were too many of the creatures to fight off by himself. A solitary charge of his crowbar sent one of the undead to the ground, however, there were more to take its place as many more piled in through the front.

He backed away, crowbar in hand, until he reached the wall before the back room. His swipes were useless, they were beginning to gang up on him. Soon, the horde had overpowered him.

Lunging on top of the professor, he kicked away the creatures who were trying to snap at his legs. The stronger ones were pinning him to the ground. He could smell their putrid breath wavering into his nostrils.

A female zombie with tattered strips of grey hair was the first to puncture his skin. The pain was not as bad as Professor Ulrich thought it would be. His body became docile as the flock plunged its hands up and into the professor's torso, their fingers muddling inside for chunks of organs and flesh.

Led Zeppelin's "When The Levee Breaks" playing in his head, the professor closed his eyes and pictured Faith's big blue eyes staring at him lovingly.

$$* \quad * \quad * \quad *$$

Faith's demise began after the front-store feast had ended. She sat in the darkness, her mind set on the fact that both her ex-husband and Dane succumbed to the death grips of the undead army.

Her mind was halfway in denial, thoughts of her wedding day still running rampant throughout her brain. "I love you, Bruce," she said to herself. She dropped the hammer to the floor and brought her hands to her face.

Her blonde hair in her face, Faith ran her hands up and down her cheeks, feeling the moist residue of her salty tears from earlier.

She heard the horrible noises outside the back room door. There were no more moans, only the sounds of sloppy chewing and sucking. Those noises ceased when she heard footsteps dragging their way to Faith's reclusive area.

When hands burst through the cheap wood of the door, Faith's tears signified the final drops of her life in this world.

CHAPTER 28

▼

Nathan clenched his teeth as he felt around the wound on his shoulder. Bits of blood were beginning to drip again from the deep cut, but the heavy flow had stopped minutes ago.

Dez looked past the construction site at the flickering flames in the distance. His mind was still fixated on what could have possibly occurred in the area. He felt the sweat soak his shirt; he pulled it at and it peeled away from his skin.

Nathan leaned off of the workman's bench and nearly slipped on the wet ground below his boots. He removed his hand from his wound and looked around the area for a weapon. He quickly settled on an orange-plated nail gun that was lodged on one of the lower shelves. Checking it for a loaded clip, he brought it back behind his head and looked at his brother and Chester, who were silent.

"We can't keep running," said Dez, who banged the bench with the metal pipe. "There could be even more devastation beyond this point. We could see what caused that explosion a few miles down and be confronted with thousands of those monsters instead of the hundreds we just ran away from." He spit on the ground.

Chester kicked a bit of mud away from him and sighed. "You're right, Dez," he began. "It either ends here or we keep running, and running isn't exactly the best idea at this point. We have to hope that the transit will be ending soon. Look, you can see the sunlight starting to peek through the night sky." He pointed upwards, and the other two slowly turned their heads in the direction.

Dez began to walk towards the first row of steel beams in the condominium complex. As he swung his arm around one, he heard Nathan start to feel the latest tinges of pain from his deadly wound. At that moment, he wanted to take the ache from his brother and add it to his already blackened heartbreak.

He walked over to Nathan and butted his head with him. "Little bro," he started, fighting away the sorrow in his system. They both knew the fight was an oncoming storm of macabre. Chester joined in, throwing his arms around the two.

It was then that they heard the moans in the distance.

"Here we go, they're coming." Chester backed away from Dez and Nathan and picked up the jagged piece of metal he had been eying on the soft, muddy ground. He felt its sharp, rigid edges and figured it was a viable weapon.

Dez was attacked without warning when a creature emerged from the darkness of the construction site. "Shit!" he shouted as the intruder pummeled him to the ground.

Face filled with mud, he swiped the monster's face with his elbow, sending it backwards. Chester quickly lunged at it, tackling it to the ground. As mud was splashed backwards, he found himself with the weight of the creature on top of him.

One shot of the nail gun was all Nathan needed to send it reeling backwards. Dez could hear the ping of the nail as it traveled through the ghoul's head and into a beam somewhere in the complex.

Nathan smiled and grabbed Chester's arm, bringing him to a standing position. "Nice shot, Nate," said Chester as he wiped streaks of mud from his pants. His attention was diverted once more when he heard the sloshing of puddles near the entrance to the construction site.

"Fuck, I see about ten of them." Dez ran up to the rest of his group and pulled them back to where he was just getting up from the ground. He tugged on Nathan's shirt, forcing his brother to kneel in the inch-deep mud puddle near the first set of steel beams.

Dez heard the slosh of kicking behind him. Drooling a thick brown liquid, the creature stood much taller than the human. It grabbed Dez by the throat and pinned him to the ground. Nathan pumped two quick nail shots, but both were lost in the thick cadaver's torso region. It looked over at Nathan before attempting to tear apart his brother.

Chester joined the action and pummeled the monster's back with his piece of jagged-edged metal. It groaned in pain and fell backwards. Dez stood to his feet and brought the pipe down on its face not once, but many times. He continued to swing at the dark bloody mess even after it ceased to fight back.

The oncoming horde had made their way to the construction site. Their deformed, decrepit hands shaped into finger-like claws, they were hungry and ready to rip apart the three members of the group.

Nathan fired a few shots into the air, some striking the creatures, other missing by mere inches. It was tough to aim with his shoulder in searing pain.

Dez felt the rage encompass his body, clenching the metal pipe tighter and tighter in his hands. Chester pulled him back. "Move back, move back!" he shouted, shoving Dez into the dark recess of the condo complex. "Nathan! Fall back!"

Nathan trotted backwards to his brother and Chester. "What are we doing?" he asked, clearly out of breath.

Chester grabbed Nathan by the front of his t-shirt and hid him in the dark behind one of the beams. "If we're going to fight, let's have it on our terms. Fuck fighting out in the light; let's draw them into here, into the dark. If we can hold them off long enough, the transit might conclude." His eyes reflected the grudge between him and the creatures.

Dez looked up into the sky. He couldn't tell where Venus' position was against the sun. He was in no position to call or estimate the remainder of the transit. He knew the group's only option was to fight and survive the remaining course of the evening.

The light bulbs refracting light off of their weapons, the three stood in silence, waiting for the multitude of zombies to reach their area.

Chester caught a separate group approaching the construction site. Upon their arrival, they stood in the center of a puddle, anxiously awaiting signs of noise from their prey. "I have an idea," he whispered to Dez, moving slowly towards the group of creatures. As he took each step, he reached up and unhinged the aluminum stitches holding the long strand of light bulbs to the bottom of the second floor of beams within the complex.

Careful to make minimal noise, he tossed the strand of bulbs over his back, levitating them high enough as to not drag along the wet ground. When he approached the undead flock, he reached down and tossed a rock into the puddle.

The enraged monsters began to move forward, sinking further into the deep puddle. Chester stepped forward and spun, letting the strand of light bulbs fly into the air and into the water. The first of the bulbs immediately burst from the spark, while the wire, which was now enveloped by the dark water, began to electrocute the creatures.

The smell of burnt, rotten flesh emaciated the cool, summer night's air. The scent immediately traveled to Dez and Nathan, who felt the putrid smell invade their nasal regions. The two backed away from the scene as Chester caught up with them.

As he stepped near them, two creatures tackled Chester, pinning him against a beam. He could feel the cold metal against his back.

"Get off me!" he bellowed, trying to push the attackers off of his body. Before Dez and Nathan could help their friend, they were sideswiped by the remaining creatures. Dez immediately swing his pipe at the first one who lunged at him. Nathan took the remaining nail gun clip out of his back pocket and tried to load it into the gun, but was halted by three zombies, who dove at him, sending the tool to the ground a few feet away from his body.

Dez tried to fight his way to his brother, but was pushed back by his attackers. He ducked down to avoid the swiping arms, who were grabbing at him for a bite. He saw the rage in their eyes as he kneeled beneath the monsters.

Nathan reached for the nail gun, but it was kicked away by the oncoming horde of zombies. He threw a punch at a female zombie who had lunged at his throat. The ghoul fell back as blood stained his knuckles.

Chester felt their hands dig into his side. His throat held back and his head flush with the beam, his fighting was useless. A sharp pain filled his left side, and he felt the creatures' greedy fingers burrow through his insides. He screamed in pain, the only thing that could be heard over the evil's hungry moans.

Dez could see his brother fall to the ground, but failed to reach the spot of the intrusion. His pipe was connecting with the few creatures that were surrounding him. He felt a sense of success whenever the metal clanged with the skull of a monster.

Dez threw down the metal pipe and stiff-armed the creature in front of him. It went barreling backwards into others, creating a small pile on the muddy ground.

He heard Chester's continuous screams as he inched closer to his brother. When he turned around, the squeals halted. He no longer saw his best friend pinned against the steel beam. Instead, he saw a familiar sight for the evening: the creatures were huddled around in a near-perfect circle, their foul heads bobbing up and down in feeding glory.

Dez swallowed a large lump in his throat. Chester was now dead.

He saw Nathan fighting away the mass of ghouls that had him cornered. As he furthered his way to his brother, he was quickly brought to the ground. He tasted the sour mud in his mouth, spitting out whatever he could.

Dez kicked his attacker in the face, but slipped as he tried to stand. He once again fell to the ground, this time with a set of hands grabbing at his stomach. Two more entered the fray, and he was surrounded by them. He brought his arms in front of his face and spun his body, letting his shin connect with one of the zombies.

The largest one of the group held him to the ground and dug its fingers into his cheeks. Before it could pierce his pale skin, it fell backwards, landing on Dez's legs. He leaned up and turned around. All he could hear was the shots being fired out of the nail gun. He ducked his head back into his arms and tried not to swallow or breathe in any of the wet mud beneath his face.

Each nail penetrated their heads perfectly, sometimes hitting the creatures right between their black, malevolent eyes. Nathan pumped the remaining shots into one of them that was about to lunge at him from behind a beam.

Dez reached a standing position and ran over to his brother. As soon as he threw his arms up to embrace him, Nathan fell to the ground. Dez leaned down and could see that most of the flesh garnering his throat had been ripped away. "I was overpowered," Nathan spoke, his words traveling out of mouth with droplets of blood. "I couldn't fight all of them at once."

Nathan placed a hand over his throat and the other gripped Dez's hand. "Nathan, stay with me, bro," he began. "I saw an elevator lift inside the complex. We can ride it to the roof and wait out the transit." He could feel his brother compress his fingers within his own.

Dez put his head down on Nathan's chest. "Stay with me, little brother, I'm not going to let you go." His vision was marred with tears.

Dez floated out of reality. Flashes of his life with Nathan and Chester flickered in and out of his mind. He recalled fixing his brother's bowtie before sending him in his limo before Nathan's senior high school prom. Careless days were filled with late nights at the apartment, drinking beer and playing Metallica too loud over the living room sound system.

Dez felt himself sitting in the comfortable couch in living room, laughing and feeling great about life. Chester was sitting across from him in the recliner, feet up and a frosty bottle of cold beer in his hand. Nathan would often crack the group up by making obvious comments during Red Sox games.

The blood was continuing to flow out of Nathan's throat wound. He looked up at Dez, who felt his serine stare pierce his soul. "Big bro," Nathan gurgled. "What would I do without you?" He smiled a large grin, showing his white teeth.

Dez let his tears come down. "Nathan, don't go," he barely got out. He pulled harder on his brother's hand. The smile left Nathan's face as he passed on. He died without crying, his brown eyes still wide open, looking up at the sky.

Dez brought Nathan up to his chest, giving his brother one final hug. He wiped the tears from his eyes and placed his arms across his chest. Before leaving him, he gently pushed his eyelids down over his eyes.

More of the undead were oncoming towards the scene. Dez clenched his teeth and picked up the metal pipe he had thrown to the ground earlier. The slower moving creatures reached for him, but he pushed them away.

Dez walked over to the elevator lift and knelt down on its red metallic base. He let the pipe drop and clang against the floor. He reached his arms over the side of the lift's handles and pushed down the button on the wire's control box.

The tears had ended. Dez watched as the ghouls lumbered over to the construction site, some with arms outstretched, others moving a more rapid pace. He did not want to think that they would feed on the remains of both Chester and Nathan.

The lift moved up, making an echoing grunt as it passed by each floor of the condominium complex. Dez turned around and stared at each line of bulbs, letting their light soothe his tired eyes. He looked past the outset of the complex and into the flames a mile away, which were still burning, but not as brightly as before.

In matter of mere hours, Dez had lost the three most important people in this life. He looked up the sky, which was bearing down on him, unapologetic for the uncompromising massacre it had brought upon Dez that evening.

Further past the night sky, Venus was rounding out its transit with the sun and the earth. The alignment was beginning to end.

CHAPTER 29

▼

Dez peered over the edge of the lift. As he passed by each floor of the condominium complex, surges of memories blazed within the recesses of his mind. He saw Koral standing against a steel beam, smiling at him, as if to mock him for breaking his heart.

His parents were on the next floor; his father grinning at him and his mother waving. Chester sat on the next floor, flipping through a magazine, only nodding to acknowledge Dez as he passed by him.

Johnny raised a bottle of beer to him on the floor after, using his other hand to give him devil horns. The lift approached the floor before the roof. Nathan stood there, his arms outstretched.

"Hey big bro," he said as Dez stared into the empty space. Nathan let his arms fall as the lift's ride came to a halt.

Dez stepped off the lift and onto the roof. The metal clanged under his thick black boots as he walked forward. Each step he took was another memory, reinforcing the quandaries of the life he once owned; now just mere flashes of the past, he sighed and continued to walk forward.

The night sky was beginning to fade away. Dez looked up at the sun. Although he could not see the black dot of Venus collude with the edge of the sun, he knew it was there. He thought of when Professor Ulrich first explained the transit to him at Vincenzo's. He remembered the Motley Crue song playing in the background, that Hannah chick waiting for him at the bar.

His feet still clanging against the metal floor, Dez slowed his pace as he approached the opposite edge of the roof. He could smell the smoke from the once apparent flames from the explosion earlier in the night. He wondered what was going on past the chaos.

Dez made it to the edge of the roof. Even thought he had an extreme fear of heights, he knelt down and then fell back, throwing his feet over the side. Both boots swung back and forth, hundreds of feet into the air over the ground. "You look so beautiful," he said to the visions in the sky.

Dez could see the destruction of the city from so high up. Revmont was a dump before the chaos, he thought, but it looked like an ancient romantic city compared to the destruction he viewed from the edge of the roof.

Only 24 hours ago, life was considerably different. He was stuck in the vicious circle of heartbreak, a victim of Koral's inability to love. He concentrated so much on how his life was affected by one person and began to laugh out loud. His laughter echoed throughout the complex, the only human sounds being eradiated.

He heard Chester's distinguishing chuckle in the background of his mind, followed by the sounds Nathan used to make when he air-drummed to a song. He heard the clink of glasses being shoved together with Johnny. He heard the sound of silence next.

Dez could make out the water tower at the opposite side of the city near Revmont Beach. It too, was in flames, perhaps as a means of defense or a result of devastation. Across the way, the smoke filtered in with the remnants of the crisp summer night air.

"Hello, Revmont," Dez whispered to himself, his hands tightly gripped within the edge of the roof.

He wondered if Johnny was still alive, maybe the professor and Faith had found medical help and were sitting in an emergency station somewhere, they themselves wondering if he, Chester and Nathan had survived the night.

Or, maybe they were dead. After all, it would not make a difference in the least. If the transit ended and the dimension of the dead were closed once again, it would not matter.

Dez was already dead. He had no heart; he had not a drop of soul left in his body.

Breathing in, Dez looked up at the sky. Specks of blue were beginning to take over the darkness, pushing away the black to make room for the sun once more. That black sky had shaped his world.

Epilogue

▼

Peeking from the broken shards of green-painted wood, the man reached his head out of the small opening. Sunlight had been pouring into his hideout for a few minutes now.

He had been hiding out in his basement all evening. When the word first traveled to him, he was on his way home from work at the gas station. He was only a short distance away from his house; when he got there he rushed into the bedroom to find his wife locked in the closet. She greeted him with the most embracing hug he had ever received.

Wiping the basement's dust off his white and red stitched "Jasper" nametag, he called down to his wife. "Honey! Everything's fine up here!" he shouted as the bright sunlight gleamed directly into his eyes.

"Ok, Jasper!" she shouted from the corner of the basement.

As he knelt down, he took a deep breath. He couldn't believe they had done it: they had survived the night.

He raised his arms and stretched, yawning as he began to smile. He tilted his head back and sighed. The bright sunlight continued to pour over him.

He smelled the rotten breath behind him, followed by unearthly hungry moaning. He turned around and immediately felt its teeth digging into his flesh.

0-595-34439-9

Printed in the United States
27718LVS00003B/220

9 780595 344390